MW00878551

CYNTHIA HICKEY

ANYTHING
FOR A
MYSTERY
A Nosy Neighbor Mystery, Book 1
By Cynthia Hickey

To God and my family who give me the encouragement to write..

ACKNOWLEDGMENTS

Thank you to my readers who are always eagerly
awaiting the next mystery..

1

Tromping through the dark was not on my list of favorite things.

My flashlight's beam barely cut through the black of a moonless night. Why did I, Stormi Nelson, New York Times bestselling author and all-around scaredy-cat, volunteer to head up the neighborhood watch program? I could've been upstairs in my renovated Victorian, glass of wine in hand, plotting out my next romance novel. But no, I'd gone and opened my big mouth. Now, I wandered the scary night street.

It didn't matter that I lived in a gated community. Evil could scale fences.

What sounded like a shriek came from my left. I whirled, shining my thin ray of light into the bushes. A cat yowled and dashed past my feet. Yep, definitely not my thing. Bad things lurked outside my house. I read it in books, newspapers, and on television, even wrote about it in my books. I experienced it firsthand five years ago with the death of my father.

There ought to be something else a reclusive author could do to contribute to society. But no, my all-knowing agent suggested I mingle more to prevent my characters from becoming cardboard cutouts. Said I needed fresh fodder for my stories. Ugh. Can't I squeeze in a couple hours of reality television and call it a day? Rely on someone else's observations of the human species to feed my creativity?

Maybe I should've moved to a remote cabin in the mountains instead of the classy, gated community I chose. Oh, but I love my house. I love its turrets and balconies and original wood floors. The stuff romances are made of, minus the handsome hero, unfortunately.

A dog barked. The sound cut through the night and increased in intensity. With my heart in my throat, and perspiration coating my forehead, I slid through an opening in the nearest hedge and headed toward the sound. After all, neighborhood watch people are supposed to, well, watch the neighborhood, right? Investigate anything suspicious?

I stepped off the sidewalk and into a pile of noxious smelling mushiness. By the odor, nobody needed to tell me someone's pet left their calling card and that it now stuck to the bottom of my shoe. Definitely a point to be brought up at the next neighborhood gathering. Grimacing, I wiped the bottom of my sneaker in a lush pile of grass and continued toward the frantic animal. Before I reached my destination, the dog gave a shrill yelp, and then went silent. Nothing stirred. No leaves rustled. No birds chirped. The hair on my arms stood at attention.

Crouching, I waddled closer to where I'd heard the animal. Maybe it was hurt. My flashlight illuminated green eyes from the recesses of an Igloo style dog house.

"What's the matter, sweetie? Afraid of the dark?" I inched closer, leaving the protection of the hedge. "I don't like it much myself."

The dog whined and pulled back its massive head. Before I could straighten, a step crunched behind me. Something struck me in the back of the head. I dropped my flashlight, and fell forward into probably the only mud puddle in Oak Meadow Estates.

Footsteps pounded away. I groaned, blinking against the multi-colored spots behind my eyelids. Was this what my agent had in mind when she wanted me to be more social? Somehow, I didn't think so.

With my stomach threatening to lose its contents, I pushed to my feet. Leaves crunched behind me. I dove over the fence, skirted around a mound in the yard, and scrambled into the doghouse. A tight squeeze, but it beat the alternative of being attacked again.

Maybe not the smartest move, ducking into a strange dog's territory, but the poor pooch seemed as scared as I was. I wasn't too afraid of being bitten, at this point. We cowered together and waited until silence once again filled the spring night.

I tangled my fingers in the thick, coarse fur of my new best friend. "I feel a little foolish, kiddo, but someone clunked me in the head. I bet I have a huge goose bump back there. There's no blood, is there?" I gingerly felt the spot right above my spine. No blood.

"So, buddy, what do we do now? Shouldn't you be out there growling and warning off two-legged predators? Keeping me safe?" It didn't appear I could do much for myself in that area.

The dog woofed low in his throat.

"A fine time to show a little backbone." I crawled to the door and peered outside. Since I'd dropped my flashlight, I couldn't see a thing. I shoved my hand into the pouch of my hoodie and withdrew my cell phone. Three key punches later, the 9-1-1 operator answered.

"9-1-1, what is your emergency?"

"Somebody attacked me and hit me in the back of the head."

"Did you lose consciousness?"

"No." At least I didn't think so.

"Did you get a look at your assailant?"

"No." Didn't I say they hit me from the back?

"Where are you now?"

"I'm … in a dog house on Pine Street." This conversation was going nowhere fast.

"A dog house?"

"I hid in here." I rubbed the back of my neck, my wish for something cold to drink stronger than ever before. "Look. I'm going home. Can you please send an officer? I'd wait here, but I really hate the dark." I cut off my rambling and gave the woman my address on Hickory Road and crawled from the confining space. "See you later, new friend." With another glance to make sure no one waited to clobber me again, I ran home as fast as my wobbly legs would carry me.

Being quiet by nature, violence of any kind never failed to take me by surprise. Tears burned the back of my eyelids. There was a reason I wrote romance and not crime novels. With a sniff, I slammed and locked my front door behind me and made a beeline for my refrigerator.

Glass of wine poured, I tossed rice, butter, French onion soup, and chicken breasts in a nine-by-thirteen-inch pan and tossed it in the oven. I wasn't sure when cooking became my escape from the world, but the overstocked freezer in the garage attested to the fact I cooked way more than I could eat.

My cats, Ebony and Ivory, twined around my legs as I moved to the living room and stared out the plate glass window that covered most of one wall. Where were the police? It occurred to me, for a second, that maybe I shouldn't stand in front of the window, but I decided tonight's attack was simply a case of being in the wrong place at the wrong time. What were the odds the attacker knew my name, much less where I lived? Besides, I hadn't done anything more than take an evening stroll.

No. I sipped my Chablis. I'd stumbled upon someone up to no good while I made my rounds for the Neighborhood watch, reinforcing my desire to rarely venture from the safety of my house.

A tantalizing smell of butter and onions drifted from the kitchen at the same time a dark sedan pulled into my curved driveway. I stepped behind the curtain and peered around the edge. Hopefully, the tall, muscular figure who slid from the car and marched toward the house was a police officer and not a bad guy. The doorbell rang, answering my question. After all, whoever heard of a crook ringing the bell?

I took a deep breath, exhaled hard enough to puff out my cheeks, and opened the door. "Yes?"

"Ma'am. I'm Detective Steele. You called about an assault?"

They sent a detective? I expected a routine cop. I stepped back and opened the door wide enough for him to enter. One look at him in the light and my breath caught. He towered over my five-feet-five inches by about a foot. Hair the color of ripe wheat was combed back from a face that ought to grace the cover of my romance novels. His eyes were the color of my favorite comfort food—chocolate.

I patted my stick straight hair for flyaways. "Yes, I'm, um, Stormi Nelson."

He smiled. "The author. My sister loves your books."

"She does?" I lifted my glass and tried to give an alluring peek over the rim. Spending so much time in my own company didn't exactly teach me proper flirtation techniques. Except for the ones I used in my novels, anyway, and I made most of those up. My mother said nobody acted that silly in real life.

The conk on the head must've knocked me loopy, considering I forgot my manners. "Please, come in." I waved him toward the only chair in the parlor.

Detective Steele pulled a small spiral notebook from his shirt pocket and sat in my leather easy chair. His eyes widened as he looked around the sparsely furnished room. "Did you just move in?"

"No." I dragged in a lawn chair from the dining room. "I rarely use any room but my bedroom and office. Never saw the sense in furnishing rooms I rarely use."

He shook his head. "You told the operator someone hit you over the head and you, uh, hid in a dog house."

"Yes." I sipped my wine. "I'm head of our neighborhood watch." An element of pride laced my words. "Today was my turn to patrol." Actually, every night would be until someone else volunteered." I heard a dog barking so I went to investigate. When I did, someone hit me. I scrambled to safety inside an igloo."

His lips thinned. "Did you happen to see the body you tripped over?"

I coughed, spewing my drink across my lap. "Excuse me?"

"The dog you spent time with had an owner. An owner, that according to clues at the scene, you tripped over." His eyes probed mine.

"I, oh!" I remembered the shapeless lump on the ground. "It's dark outside. I didn't know it was a body, and I'm certain I walked *around* it." With a shaky hand, I set my glass on an unpacked cardboard box. The thought I might have actually touched a dead body, left me trembling. "Do you think whoever hit me killed that person? What about the dog? What's going to happen to it? It was scared to death." The poor thing couldn't stay there alone. A flush of guilt washed over me as I realized I might appear to care more about an animal than a person. "This is tragic."

"Miss Nelson—"

"Do you think I killed somebody?" I clutched my throat and leaped to my feet. "I'm an author, not a murderer!" Good Lord, he was here to arrest me. "I only kill people on paper, or I will soon, anyway."

"Miss Nelson—"

"Am I a suspect? Do I need a lawyer?" I didn't know one. How would I go about hiring a reputable attorney? I've only lived here a few months. My throat threatened to swell shut with suppressed tears. "How did you know which dog house I hid in?"

"I'm only here to ask some questions, Miss Nelson. Did you obtain medical attention for your injury?"

"No. It's just a bump on the head. I mean, I fell to my knees, got a little sick to my stomach, but other than some mud on my favorite jogging pants, no harm done. Should I go?"

"It might add credibility to the fact you attest to being struck."

My eyes widened, and I bent my head forward. "Here. Feel. There's a bump as big as your fist."

"No need." After I glanced up, he handed me a business card. "Please come down to the station in the morning and fill out a report. If you don't show up, I'll be back to arrest you. If I have more questions, I'll contact you." With another shake of his head, he stood and strode past me without answering a single one of *my* questions.

Wonderful. Now, he could go home and tell his sister that her favorite romance author was a complete nutcase and possible murder suspect. I sank into the chair he'd vacated and buried my flaming face in my hands.

Within minutes, my doorbell rang again. One peek out the window showed Detective Steele. I sniffed and answered the door. "Yes?"

He handed me a leash. Attached to the leash was the wiriest-haired mutt I'd ever seen. "This is the deceased neighbor's dog. I was going to take her to the pound until we found a relative willing to take her, but your concern told me you might be the better choice."

"I can keep her?" My heart leaped.

"Well, temporarily, at least. The tag on her collar says her name is Sadie. I think she's an Irish Wolfhound."

Ebony and Ivory wouldn't be happy, but I was ecstatic. The poor dog wasn't the prettiest thing, but we'd shared an adventure together. "Thank you."

"Good night, Miss Nelson." He nodded and headed to his car.

"Good night, Detective," I whispered as I closed the door. I sure wished I'd have met the handsome officer under different circumstances. Somehow, being a suspect in a murder investigation did not lend a romantic tone to a meeting.

I'd no sooner pulled my casserole from the oven before headlights flashed through my window. I sighed and wished again for a cabin in the woods. I parted the curtains and frowned.

Why was there a U-Haul truck in my driveway?

2

Hoping Sadie might be braver with me beside her, and thus willing to protect me from harm, I stepped onto my front porch. After all, her sheer size ought to make a person think twice about approaching the house. A mini van pulled in behind the U-Haul. My mother, older sister, niece, and nephew bounded from the vehicles. My heart dropped to my toes.

"Darling!" My mother spread her arms.

"Mom? What are all of you doing here? Do you know what time it is?" I swallowed against the boulder in my throat.

"Of course." She enveloped me in a bear hug, suffocating me with Taboo cologne. "It's ten-thirty. Sorry, we're late. Traffic, you know." With a kiss on my cheek that most likely left an imprint of her favorite fuchsia-colored lipstick, she breezed into the house.

My sister, Angela, tossed me a grin and ushered her sullen-faced teens, Cherokee and Dakota, ahead of her. I officially died and went to hell. "Come on, Sadie. Maybe it isn't as bad as I fear."

"This is perfect." Mom twirled in my foyer.

Things were definitely as bad as I feared. "What

do you mean?" Don't say what I think you're going to say.

"It's a good thing I brought my furniture. There's nowhere to sit. These huge rooms are screaming to be decorated. I'm quite good at home décor, you know. People are always telling me how inviting my home is." She stopped dancing and smiled. "I've sold my condo in Boca Raton. Your sister's divorce is final. Three gorgeous single women living in a glorious house. Won't this be fun?" She flitted from room to room like a deranged hummingbird. "We couldn't see much of the neighborhood because it's so dark, but it looks fabulous! We're going to be so happy here."

She said my fear out loud. What about me being happy? I tightened my hold on Sadie; my anchor to sanity. "I don't have beds, linens, towels, nothing for all of you. Mom, you should've called."

Her face fell. "You don't want us here?"

"It's not that." How would I get any work done? I needed to change tactics, and fast. "It isn't a safe neighborhood for kids." That'd get her. She doted on her grandchildren. "I was attacked today not one block from here."

Mom narrowed her eyes and tilted her head. "You look fine."

"I was hit over the head. The cops just left."

"You poor dear." I found myself smothered again. "I'll sleep with you tonight. Just in case you have a seizure or something. You know what they say about knocks on the head. You could have a concussion. Your sister and the kids can use the sleeping bags in the van. Tomorrow, we'll set your house to rights. Maybe even throw a housewarming party. I love parties."

Yep. I was definitely paying for some grievous sin committed in my past.

"Cherokee is allergic to dogs," Angela said, grimacing at Sadie. Ebony and Ivory chose that moment to streak by. "And cats. She can't sleep on the floor." She glanced at her son who was busy tapping away on a handheld computer game console. "Dakota can sleep anywhere."

"Then Cherokee will have to curl up in my one chair. The animals were here first." I unclipped Sadie's leash and led the dog to the kitchen while the others traipsed back outside. "Poor thing. You must be thirsty. It's been a stressful night." I filled a mixing bowl with water and set it on the floor.

Maybe I shouldn't be so put out about my family moving in, but, they should've at least called first. How will I get any writing done with kids in the house? Or my mother and her parties. I hadn't forgotten her weekly bridge games and pink poker nights. Surely Angela would look for a job. What then? Stormi the babysitter? Not likely. The cats were already hissing, growling, and skirting wide circles around the dog. They'd be over-the-wall traumatized by a house full of people.

"Sadie, what did you think of the hunky Detective Steele?" I said, determined to dwell on more pleasant thoughts as I leaned against the counter. "I would've liked to have met him under different circumstances. Of course, then I probably wouldn't have had the nerve to carry on a conversation. Not that I excelled at it tonight." But it was nice of him to bring me the dog. Maybe no one else would want Sadie. Maybe the giant of a canine would be my new muse. The shadow that followed me everywhere. My best friend.

Guaranteed, Sadie would accompany me on my weekly scouts around the neighborhood. A chicken or not, her size ought to deter any more people from getting close enough to hit me.

The proverbial light bulb went off over my head. Maybe it was time to move away from romances and on to writing mysteries. This could be a sign from God. I could still implement romance. The night's happenings would make the perfect springboard for me to begin, and I'd model the hero after Detective Steele. "Sadie, tomorrow, we're going back to the place it all began." After all, I would need to take notes for my finest novel yet.

*

For the first time that I could remember, I gave thanks my family were late sleepers. Not that I got any sleep next to my mother who snored like a chainsaw. The sooner she unloaded her bed, the better. If they woke as early as I did, it'd be impossible for me to sneak out without company. I slipped my feet into slippers and darted down the stairs, Sadie at my heels. My flannel pants and tee-shirt were perfectly respectable for taking a dog for a walk at seven a.m. No one would suspect a thing.

I snagged the leash from under the leather chair. Cherokee rolled over and grunted. When she didn't wake, I released the breath I held, clipped the leash to Sadie's collar, and then tiptoed out the front door.

A few people were out, doing what early risers

do. Collect the paper, take out the garbage, walk their Chihuahuas. The delicate scent of honeysuckle drifted on a light breeze. No one seemed to pay me undue attention except raise a hand in greeting, which I returned. I couldn't look suspicious.

Yellow crime scene tape surrounded the back yard of the house I'd visited. Sad in its wavy journey across a lawn covered in weeds and mid-calf high grass. Sadie barked, and I put a hand on her muzzle. We turned down the alley. When I spotted the doghouse, I paused to study the ground. Where had I seen the shadowy mound? There, or there? Why wasn't a chalk figure drawn in the grass? Isn't that what the crime scene investigators did?

"Okay, girl. I'm leaving it up to you to find me inside the house." I nonchalantly let the leash slide out of my hands. Sadie took off around the corner of the house like a rocket. I glanced around. "Oh, no. She yanked free."

"She did, did she?"

I squealed and whirled as Detective Steele emerged from the bushes. "You scared me." I planted my fists on my hips.

"Sorry." He crossed his arms and studied me with those delicious eyes. "What are you doing here, Miss Nelson?"

"Um," I twirled a strand of hair around my finger and tried to ignore the fact that I stood in front of him wearing wrinkled pajamas. "Looking for the dog's dish. Yeah."

"Then why would you tell the dog to find you a way inside the house?" He motioned his head toward a stainless steel bowl next to the back stairs. "Look. You can't be here. This is a crime scene. Your being here and wanting to get inside might put you a notch up on the suspect list."

My heart skipped a beat, and not in the good, oh he's so handsome kind of way. "I'm just walking my dog. That's not against the law."

"Miss Nelson." He frowned and raked a hand through his hair.

"Call me Stormi, please." Especially if I was going to run into him every time I turned around. "Aren't y'all finished here, anyway?"

"I'm investigating a murder. I won't be finished for a while." A muscle twitched in his jaw.

"Me too!" Something we had in common.

"I thought you were walking your dog." He crossed his arms, making the muscles in his arms bulge against his tee-shirt.

"Oh, all right." I slapped my thigh to call Sadie over when I spotted her rooting beneath a bush. "I'm going to write a mystery novel about what happened to me, and the dead body, and wanted to take notes. Whatever I couldn't find out by coming and talking to neighbors, I'd make up."

He grabbed my elbow and pulled me into the shade of a large oak tree. A delightful scent of musk teased my nostrils and I leaned a little closer to him. "A murder occurred here last night. You were allegedly attacked. It isn't the smartest idea for you to start nosing around."

O-kay. He thinks it's one of the neighbors. That was no more pleasant than him thinking I was the culprit. The hair on the back of my neck stood at attention, and I pulled back from sniffing him. Maybe I'd gather more clues by getting to know the people who lived around me. Ugh. Talk to people I didn't know?

But I'd do almost anything for research that couldn't be found on the internet. Anything for a story and all that, right? "Who do you think it is?"

He groaned. "Go home, Miss … Stormi." He grabbed Sadie's leash and handed her over to me. "And don't forget to go to the station to fill out a report."

Mulling over the unsuccessful last half hour, I tugged Sadie's leash so we could continue our exercise while my mind leaped into hyper-drive. Detective Steele had stepped from the bushes. Was he hiding or searching for something? He could be a dirty cop. How could I get back over there without getting caught? I didn't even know the dead neighbor's name. Some crime-solver I was.

Two houses over, I spotted an elderly woman wearing a high-lighter-yellow-colored housecoat. She hummed as she watered a bed of petunias and rose bushes. Spotting me, she waved. "Hello. I'm Marion Henley. You're the new neighbor over on Hickory."

"Yes." I might as well start asking questions, and this woman seemed eager to welcome me. "I'm Stormi Nelson. It's nice to meet you."

"Yes, yes, we're all a twitter over the new author on the block." She moved her dentures back and forth with her tongue. "I ain't talking about excitement, you understand." She peered at me over wire-rimmed glasses. "I'm talking about that newfangled thing on the computer that folks use to communicate. Twitter. The gossip is flying back and forth faster than a bee's wings."

The neighbors are talking about me? My smile faded.

"We don't all take too kindly to a romance novel writer on the street. No telling what kind of things goes on in your house in the name of research." She leaned forward and lowered her voice. "But personally, I'm not averse to a little bodice ripping once in awhile, if you know what I mean."

I literally didn't know what to say.

Marion splashed some water on the sidewalk for Sadie to lap up. "I guess you've heard about the tragedy at Ethel's."

I perked up. "Ethel?"

"Yeah. My neighbor. Ethel Lincoln" Marion picked up a large set of pruning shears. "Seems she was stabbed in the back with these, and you have her dog." She chuckled at my shocked look. "Not these in particular, but stabbed with shears. Last night. She doesn't have any family so no one knows if anything was taken." Snip. A faded rose fell to the ground. "My opinion … someone wanted to Shut. Her. Up."

I took a step back from the potential weapon in her hands. "What do you mean?"

"Well, she's filed about one too many complaints with the Home Owners Association. This person's grass is too long, that one doesn't take their garbage can back by six, the list is endless. My opinion … she sicced the HOA on somebody with a secret to hide." Marion winked at me. "We aren't the perfect community we appear to be."

3

I completed the rest of the walk home in a state of shock. One of my neighbors was a murderer and the rest, if Mrs. Henley was any indication, were most likely just plain nuts. I stopped two doors down and stared at my house.

What was Detective Steele doing in front of my house and why was he carrying boxes? I moved to the edge of the driveway and stared as he laughed at something Mom said. If I thought he looked good last night in pants and a shirt and tie, he looked gorgeous in jeans and a tee shirt. Funny how I hadn't noticed when I saw him half an hour ago. Too busy covering up my lie for being at the crime scene, I supposed.

"What's going on?" I held tight to Sadie's leash as she tried to rip my arm out of its socket in her attempt to welcome Detective Steele.

"Matthew here is one of our neighbors," Mom gushed. "He saw us working and offered to help. We'll have things set up inside in no time."

I cringed at the sight of a flowered sateen sofa being carried through the front door. "Matthew?"

"Or Matt." Laugh lines flirted around the

corners of his eyes. "I live one block over. I'm off duty today; saw your mother struggling with a box, so I offered my services."

I nodded and narrowed my eyes. Off duty and still snooping around the dead lady's house? Something was fishy in Oak Meadow Estates and the most handsome fish of all might just be a shark. A person heard about cops on the take all the time. Matthew Steele would need somebody to keep an eye on him. I mentally volunteered my services. No, just because cops were sometimes on the take in books and movies didn't make it true in life. My thoughts were ridiculous. Still, I would keep an eye on the gorgeous, I mean, suspicious, detective.

"I'll go put on a pot of coffee." I unclipped Sadie's leash and let her cavort around the workers' heels. Who knew where my mother managed to drum up help, but she did. My house fairly burst at the seams with muscled men. My nerves prickled my skin, itching to burst free. I really needed to overcome this phobia of crowds, of people, especially if I was going to nose around asking questions.

I scooped aromatic granules into the filter and pressed the on button. Soon, the wonderful smell of fresh ground coffee filled my kitchen and my stress began to melt away. Until Matt walked in and lounged, oh, so casually, against my counter.

"How's your head today?"

"Fine." I reached in the cabinet above my head for mugs. "If I don't touch it or move too fast."

"This is a beautiful house." Matt stepped closer. "I'm in the process of fixing mine up but it's more of a cottage style."

Cutting a sideways look at him, I took a step away. "My mother will manage to take away some of its beauty with her decorating."

He chuckled. "Yeah, she's got some wild-patterned furniture. It's nice of you to let them stay."

Not that I had a choice, really. "Just until they find their own place." I hoped.

"Still," he shrugged. "It's a good gesture."

Maybe, but I didn't want to talk about my family. "Why didn't you tell me Mrs. Lincoln was stabbed with pruning shears? Why didn't the killer stab me? Do you know what he hit me with?" The startled look on his face as I peppered him with questions was priceless. I bit my lip to keep from grinning.

Matt held up his hands. "Whoa. Where did you find out this information?"

I gave him my version of the Cheshire cat. "People talk. Probably more to me than they will to you, seeing as I'm a woman, and you're a cop." Coffee finished, I grabbed the pot and started pouring drinks. I handed him the first one. "Well?"

"The shears were found in the bushes. We think you were hit with a rock. We found one with a smear of blood and a few strands of hair that look like yours." He took a sip. "And we are not entitled to share information with a civilian."

"Oh, really. Then I won't share whatever I find out with you." I filled a mug for myself and marched out of the room.

He followed. "That would be impeding an

investigation. Meaning, it's against the law."

"Coffee's on!" I yelled out the front door then headed to the living room and gasped. It looked like a florist shop vomited across my hardwood floors.

Every piece of furniture was covered with flowered fabric. Even my leather armchair had a floral throw tossed across the back. I wanted to throttle my mother. "I'm going to my office."

"Stormi."

"What?"

"If you know anything, you have to tell me." Matt stopped at the bottom of the stairs and stared up at me. I had to admit it gave me a small sense of power. The fact that if I swooned I'd land in his arms didn't escape me either, but I had never swooned in my life. "Or at least another officer. Did you go fill out the report?"

Oops. "Okay." I smiled and continued to my office. Ah, sanctuary. I sank into my plush leather chair and swiveled to look out the window.

Acre lots afforded a lot of privacy but I could still make out my next door neighbors. A middle-aged couple lounging beside their pool. Raised voices drifted through my open window. A marital spat perhaps? I smiled and lifted my mug. Now that I'd decided to write a romantic mystery, I'd see sinister motives around every corner. What fun.

Mom sashayed to the fence, waved a hand in greeting. "Hello!"

The couple tossed half-hearted gestures in return, stood, and disappeared into their ranch-style house. Mom's shoulders slumped before she turned back to the house. How could someone be so mean?

Sure, Mom could be annoying, but she meant well. I set my mug down hard enough to splash the dark liquid onto my cherry wood desk.

The window to their kitchen faced my direction and from the body language and arm swinging, it looked like they still argued. I leaned forward. The chubby man wasn't going to hit his rail-thin wife, was he? I decided to keep an eye on the two while I enjoyed my morning beverage. After wiping up the spill, I propped my feet on the windowsill and crossed my ankles. This must be what my agent meant about people watching. I kind of liked being the nosy neighbor.

"Does it matter which bedrooms we all choose?" Mom stuck her head in the door.

"As long as it isn't mine."

"Gotcha." She withdrew.

My bedroom adjoined my office with the bathroom connecting to the other side. If I stood in one, I could see all the way to the other, if the doors were open. An improvement I'd designed myself. That way, if I really got to pacing while stuck writing, I had plenty of room.

My neighbors finally moved away from the window, and I scooted my chair back. I booted up my computer and jotted down notes for the new story. Then, I sent off an email to my agent letting her know the new path I'd decided to take. Hopefully, she'd be as excited about it as I was.

Loud laughter bounced up the stairs and slid under the door, pulling me away from my thoughts. Sounded like Mom already hosting her first party. It wouldn't occur to her to let the movers leave without fixing them a meal. I thought of my empty pantry and full freezer and wondered what she'd managed to throw together. Curiosity got the better of me, and I turned off my laptop and headed to the kitchen.

Most of the crowd seemed to have gathered in the backyard by then, and my sister, Angela was in her element passing out sodas and water to the men. I sent a puzzled look in my mother's direction.

"Matthew made a run for me." She waved a pizza box over her head. "I hope you didn't mind. Your purse was on the table."

I glanced at my watch … three o'clock? I'd spent more time in my office than I'd thought.

Matthew strode my way with a grin and holding a tall glass of Diet Coke. "Where'd you hide all day?"

"Working. Thanks." I closed my eyes and took a drink of icy heaven. "So, you and Mom are on a first-name basis?"

He laughed and sat on a camping stool. Seems Mom managed to collect a menagerie of seats for her impromptu gathering. "I think she's on a first-name basis with everyone here, your sister, too. Most of these guys are fellow officers, glad for a day off and willing to help."

I nodded and collapsed into the nearest lawn chair. "How long have you lived here?"

"About two years."

"How are the neighbors? I mean, are they friendly? I haven't had much of an opportunity to mingle in the few months I've been here."

"True and all the neighbors have been

speculating about you." He winked. "I convinced them you weren't a raving homicidal maniac, but haven't been able to steer them from the immoral romance author angle."

"Thanks for that. Who lives nearest to me?" I motioned to my right.

He craned his neck to peer around me. "That would be Herman and Cecelia Edgars. They stay pretty much to themselves. There are a few families in the development, people with kids around your niece's and nephew's ages. A lot of retired people and a few of us single ones."

"Anyone capable of murder?" Sadie pushed her snout under my hand. "Where you been, sweetie? Enjoying the party?"

His eyes hardened. "Everyone is capable of murder under the right circumstances."

I took a gulp of my drink and instantly recoiled in pain. Brain freeze. My face contorted.

"Put your tongue on the top of your mouth."

I did, and the roof eventually warmed. Now, people might not be my favorite animal, but I liked to believe there was more good in the human race than bad. "I disagree."

"Then I hope you never have cause to find out what you're capable of." Matt crushed his can and stood. "I'm getting another. Want anything?"

"A slice of pizza please." I admired the view as he moved away. Firm, tall, muscular, very nice back side. An alpha male. Yeah, I could see how he might be able to kill under the right circumstances. After all, he'd been trained. I hoped his weapon of choice wasn't garden tools.

Angela squealed as a burly man wrapped his arms around her and nuzzled her neck. Cherokee sashayed by with a young man hanging on her shoulders. Mom skipped by with a platter of hot wings. The only family member unaccounted for was Dakota. He'd most likely holed up somewhere with his video games since there weren't any young girls his age. It never failed to surprise me how amorous people, even strangers, seemed to get during springtime.

"Your order, madam." Matt plopped on the grass at my feet and leaned against my knees.

Okay. Kind of familiar fairly quickly, but it felt nice. I couldn't remember the last time I had a date. My heart drummed hard enough to accompany the rock song on a radio someone had brought. "Thanks." Before taking a bite of the ham and pineapple slice, I wiped my sweaty palms on my pants and let my gaze roam the crowd.

"How many of these people are my neighbors?"

"None, other than me." Matt folded his slice of meat lovers pizza and took a bite, his eyes shrewd as he studied me. "Don't get involved, Stormi. Nothing good will come from being a nosy neighbor."

Was that a threat? It sounded like one. Suddenly his close proximity didn't feel so warm. Why the interest anyway? I narrowed my eyes. Was he the killer? Did he think I knew more than I did and was thus a danger to him being caught? I scooted my chair back.

Matt fell backwards, upending his plastic cup on his chest. "Hey!"

"Ooops." I grinned and hopped to my feet. "Let me get you a towel."

"You did that on purpose."

"Why would—"

A gunshot rang out. I dove to the ground.

4

Matt threw his body over mine, smashing me into the ground and into spilled beer. "Don't move."

I unburied my face, spitting dirt and grass, and jerked back at the sight of a gun in Matt's hand. Had he carried it the whole time? I wasn't sure how I felt about a weapon on my property, but I was pretty sure it ranked low on my list. And I thought he said he was off-duty. Did off-duty cops carry a gun? Obviously, there was more to Mrs. Lincoln's death than Matt was telling me.

In the corner of the yard, Mom peered around the trunk of a huge oak tree. Cherokee lay flat on the ground like an uprooted worm. I guess she figured playing dead was her best option. Angela ran to and fro like a headless chicken until one of the moving guys tackled her to the ground.

"Who's shooting?"

"I don't know." Matt's warm breath tickled my ear. "But I aim to find out. Stay put." And he was gone, leaving me vulnerable.

Since I found myself lying in a puddle of sticky dirt, I had no intentions of being still. Inch-by-inch I sat up. Sadie bounded toward me, licked my face, and burped. A wave of beer breath washed over me. Great. A drunk giant dog. I narrowed my eyes and glanced around the yard. Who was leaving their drinks unattended?

With a gruff bark, Sadie headed toward where the shots were fired. Obviously, a little alcohol gave my dog courage.

Another shot rang out from my neighbor's place. Then a mighty rustle and squeaking and the sky grew dark from a multitude of winged creatures. "Matt, wait. Someone's shooting at bats. That's all."

He stopped his mad dash across the yard. Slowly, the party guests got to their feet and came out of hiding, all of the cops holding guns. Matt shoved his weapon back into his waistband and pulled his tee-shirt down to conceal it. The others followed suit.

Time for the party to be over. After folding my lawn chair and leaning it against the porch rail, I began cleaning up discarded cups and cans. The impromptu party I hadn't been in the mood for anyway, but ended up enjoying, lost some of its zeal after hearing gunshots. I glanced around to see Mom and Angela stuffing garbage into bags while the other guests packed up their equipment and headed for their vehicles. Matt was nowhere in sight. Hopefully, he left to give the bat killer a piece of his mind.

When Matt still hadn't returned by the time the yard was back to rights, I moved into the house. Might as well see how my mother destroyed the rest of it with her decorating.

The kitchen sported candy-apple red curtains that looked surprisingly nice with the cream-painted wooden cabinets. Someone had replaced the white plastic patio set I used as kitchen furniture with a fifties vintage-style dinette set with vinyl seats that matched the curtains. Nice.

I purposely didn't glance into the floral living room. Seen it, didn't like it, and thank the Lord, Mom didn't touch my office. I kept the door closed so she wouldn't be invited to. My bedroom still remained pine wood and white Battenberg bedding and curtains. Wonderful. Mom at least knew not to cross certain boundaries. Whatever they chose to do with their own rooms would be fine with me.

"So?" Mom stepped to my side. "Does the house meet with your approval?"

"All except the front room. What possessed you to buy so much flowered stuff?"

She shrugged. "It's homey. Welcoming."

"That's a matter of opinion."

"Don't worry. It's only until I get my own place."

Which I knew could be weeks, months, or years, depending on Mom's mood. I sighed. There's no way I'd kick my family out, and she knew it. "Good night, Mom." I leaned over and planted a kiss on her cheek. "Thanks for the party."

A smile lit up her face. "You're welcome. Biscuits and chocolate gravy for breakfast."

Just like that, all became right with my world. I practically skipped to my room and headed across the polished oak floors to close my curtains.

A light flickered in the yard behind me. Was the

bat man at it again? I peered through the glass. No, the bobbing light moved farther away. Curiosity got the best of me, and I opened the French doors to step onto my half-circle patio balcony.

Tonight wasn't any brighter than the one before and visibility was almost nonexistent. What could they be looking for after ten o'clock? I glanced at the unfriendly couple's house next door. Dark windows greeted me. If I wanted to gather clues for my new novel, I'd need to devise a way to meet my neighbors, all of them. I stepped back in the room and locked the door.

Maybe I could use the excuse of recruiting more people for the Neighborhood Watch, since the sign-up sheet was blank except for my name. I could call another meeting. No, door-to-door would work best. My stomach flipped over at the thought of initiating contact and conversation with people I didn't know. Maybe Mom would come to the door with me.

*

I stuffed a bite of chocolate-covered biscuit into my mouth and closed my eyes. Heaven. As much as I liked cooking, I enjoyed someone else serving up a delightful dish once in a while, too. I sighed and set down my fork.

"Mom, I need a way to meet the neighbors."

Angela wiped her mouth with a napkin and frowned as her kids heaped more gravy on their plates. "You could always have another party. That was fun."

"No, something more … intimate. More one-on-one."

Mom set another pan of biscuits on the table. "I

couldn't help but notice how much food you had in your freezer. Maybe you could find out which neighbors are elderly and in need."

"How would I do that? It's not like I can knock on their door and ask them how old they are."

"Ask Matt which ones might benefit from your cooking."

Good idea but it wouldn't allow me to ask questions. It's not like I could ring the door bell and say, Hey, how well did you know Mrs. Lincoln? Did you like her? Did you kill her?

"Well, y'all figure it out." Angela stood. "But why you want to know all these people is beyond me. I'm taking the kids to enroll them in school and beat the rush when other parents wait until the last minute the first week of August. See you later."

I nodded and turned back to Mom. No way around it. I'd have to let her know my plans. Once Angela left the room, I folded my arms on the table top and leaned forward. "Okay. My real reason is I've decided to write romantic mysteries. I'd like to use the crime committed a couple of nights ago as my first book. What's a clever way to get information out of people I've never met?"

"As head of the Neighborhood Watch, why don't you go around asking people about their concerns? Then you can fish for more information." Mom began stacking dishes. "Take a clipboard or something so you look official. Maybe wear a suit."

No, thank you. I'll stick to capris and gym shoes. I carried my plate to the sink and fought the urge to lick off the lingering chocolate. "Thanks, Mom, that's a great idea."

Sadie whined at my feet. "No, you can't have the chocolate either. And you aren't going on the walk with me. I can only concentrate on one thing at a time and your previous owner didn't leash train you very well." From the dog's red eyes, I'd bet she nursed one heck of a hangover. I headed upstairs to change out of my pajamas.

Ebony and Ivory meowed and stretched on top of my coverlet. The poor darlings rarely left my room since Sadie moved in. I scratched behind both their ears. "Sorry, about all the commotion, guys. But we'll all have to get used to it. No one's leaving any time soon."

I wasn't going to follow Mom's advice on the suit, but I did want to look presentable. I surveyed my sparse closet. An author's job didn't require a large wardrobe. No one saw you while you sat in your office chair, zoned out, staring at the computer screen. Most of the time I wore yoga pants and tank tops.

With a sigh, I pulled out a pair of Capri pants in stripes of sherbet colors, very summery. I chose a bubblegum pink tee shirt to go with them, slid my feet into blue glittery flip-flops, and I was ready to go.

"You look like you're six years old," Mom said as I dug some paper out of a drawer. "All you need is the clown makeup and pig tails. You really need more fashionable clothes. After all, you're an author, and need to market yourself." She always lowers her voice when she says that, like being an author is a big secret. "Your red hair clashes with those colors."

"I have an outfit I wear to book signings and conferences. That's good enough for me." I waved two sheets of lined paper at her. "Gotta go." I dashed out the door before she could remark any further on my lack of style.

Going from one neighbor's house to the next would be hard enough without worrying about my clothes. I grinned as I snapped the paper onto the fluorescent pink clipboard I found in one of my office cabinets. Folks would see me coming a mile away.

Sadie whined through the screen door as I strolled down the driveway. I really hoped she wouldn't break through the mesh and join me on Hickory Road. I turned left. Right would take me to Mrs. Henley's house, and I already knew how she felt about the victim. Besides, I didn't want to walk past the crime scene until I absolutely had to.

I hadn't gone far when I approached the sprawling ranch style house of the bat killer. Or at least I assumed it was the place since a middle-aged man in overalls and carrying a shotgun stared into the recesses of a tall oak tree.

"Good afternoon," I sang, forcing myself to forget people terrified me. Especially ones with guns. "I'm Stormi Nelson, head of the Neighborhood Watch, and I …"

"Know how to get winged creatures out of a tree short of burning down the tree?"

"No, and I'm quite sure that wouldn't …"

"Darn Detective Steele told me I can't shoot my gun in city limits." He glared at me. "What's this world coming to?"

"Well, I don't …"

"And if I have to see another bat snatch a drink out of my pool, I'll shoot 'em anyway. I swear I will."

"That sounds—a"

"Norma, come meet the new gal." His yell almost burst my eardrum. Maybe Norma would allow me to get a word in edgewise.

"I'm going to kill you, Bill." A rotund woman wearing overalls that matched her husband's, burst from a storage shed on the side of the house and marched toward us. In her hands, she carried the biggest pair of gardening shears I'd ever seen.

5

"Who in tarnation are you?" Norma snipped the shears. "'Cause if you're here to snoop around my man, you can light a fire under your rear and keep moving."

"Excuse me?" Seriously. I'd stepped into an alternate universe. Oak Meadow Estates no longer existed. Instead, somehow, someone transplanted me to a planet far, far away. I clutched my clipboard to my chest.

"Oh, I didn't stutter, girlie." She narrowed her eyes while her lump of a husband crossed his arms and glared. Really. What woman in their right mind would want Pillsbury doughboy?

I took a deep breath and a step back, then forced the words out of my mouth in a rush. "I'm the head of the Neighborhood Watch and wanted to check to make sure you're okay after the unfortunate death of Mrs. Lincoln." Wow. I think that's the most I'd ever spoken to a stranger in one sentence.

Tears welled in Bill's eyes, while Norma's face reddened. "Got what she deserved, if you ask me," she said. "Chasing around after other women's husbands."

"Uh, wasn't she, like, sixty-two?" I didn't think she could chase anyone.

"Don't matter. A cougar if I ever saw one." She motioned her head at Bill. "Look at him crying like a baby. That tells you all you need to know."

Bill shook his head. "It's very sad."

"I'm asking you to leave now, girlie." Norma grabbed her husband's arm and dragged him toward the back of the house.

That woman had motive. I wrote her name on my paper and put a giant check mark next to it, signifying she was my top suspect. So, I had Marion Henley, and Bill and Norma, who? I'd neglected to get their last names. I banged my pencil against my head. Some Nancy Drew I was.

"You taking a census?"

I squealed and tightened my grip on the clipboard before it crashed to the sidewalk.

"Sorry. Didn't mean to startle you," said a woman who looked like the model for a Barbie doll.

Maybe if I could get past the bouncing boobs in a tight spaghetti-strapped top, I might be able to answer. My gaze traveled from her scarlet tennies, over the tight jogging outfit in the same fire-engine red, to the crimson scrunchie holding back a mass of platinum hair. "No ... problem." I suddenly felt the six-year-old Mom said I resembled.

"I'm Victoria Lanham. Most people call me Torie. You're the author."

"Yes."

"What are you doing?"

"Could you stop jogging in place, please?" The bobbing of silicone-enhanced body parts made me seasick.

She giggled. "Sorry. I saw you talking to the Olsons. Strange woman, that Norma. Thinks everyone is out to steal her husband."

"Yeah, I discovered that." I clasped the clipboard to my chest, suddenly feeling inferior in a small C-cup. "I'm checking on folks after the murder."

Torie's smile faded. She spoke through clenched teeth. "Yeah, Mrs. Lincoln was a ... real nice woman. Well, see ya later!" She tossed me a wave and jiggled down the sidewalk.

I glanced at my list of names. They could all be suspects in my book. I wanted to put Torie at the top, but there was no crime in being beautiful. Sighing, I continued to the next house.

A lovely Tudor home with a devastatingly handsome detective pruning bushes in front. He glanced up and grinned. "Hey, Stormi. My sister's inside. Let me go get her. She'd love to meet you." He set down his gardening tool and dashed away. I stared so long at the view I thought someone would have to get the acetone remover to unsuper-glue my gaze from his backside.

He returned moments later with a pixie of a woman who shared his dark blonde hair and chocolate eyes. "This is Mary Ann."

Mary Ann's arms were full of books, my books. The day brightened like a sunrise. "Would you sign these, please? I'm so excited to meet you. I love your novels. They take me away and let me experience wild and crazy romance in a clean, moral way."

"I'd be honored." I followed her to the porch where she spread the paperbacks on a patio table. I'd never tire of hearing someone recite my tagline to me. While I signed to my heart's content, she left me and returned with two glasses of lemonade.

"Where's mine?" Matt frowned.

Mary Ann waved him away. "Get your own. I'm visiting with my new best friend."

I liked the sound of that. Not having had a close friend since high school, I hadn't realized how much I missed female companionship or any human contact for that matter. Ebony and Ivory, while wonderful listeners, weren't much for conversation. Sadie occasionally barked a response while I rambled, but it still wasn't enough. Now, I had a houseful of people and next to no quiet. Still, friendship sounded nice. I took a sip of the offered drink, and puckered up like a prune.

"Too sour?" Mary Ann leaped from her seat and disappeared, leaving Matt grinning at me like a Cheshire cat. When Mary Ann returned, she dumped two teaspoonfuls of sugar in my glass. "That ought to do it."

"My sister isn't much of a cook. She can't boil water without scorching the pan." Matt chose a wooden rocker and plopped muddy boots on the porch railing. "Maybe you can teach her. Your mother said you're a good cook."

"Would you?" Mary Ann clasped her hands together. "We could bond over food."

I nodded and took another drink. This one tasted like the inside of a sugar bowl with a splash of lemon for seasoning. I set the glass on the table.

"Thanks for the drink. I'd love to do lunch sometime, Mary Ann, but I've got to be going."

"What are you up to?" Matt lowered his feet with a thud. "Why the clipboard?"

"As head of the Neighborhood Watch, I'm going door-to-door to see whether any of the residents have concerns about their safety." I tilted my chin. What was it about this man that made me want to skirt around the truth?

"You're snooping." A dimple winked in his cheek.

"No, I'm not."

He made a forward motion with his fingers. "Let me see the clipboard."

"It's personal." I clutched it tighter.

"Stormi, don't make me wrestle you for it."

"Fine." I thrust it at him, not entirely certain I didn't want to wrestle.

"What's with the checkmark? You don't really think Norma killed Ethel, do you?"

"Do you have any better ideas?"

"Not at the moment. What grounds do you have?"

"She thought Ethel was after her husband."

He laughed so hard, he snorted. "She thinks everyone is after Bill. She sicced her dog on Mary Ann once when she passed on the sidewalk. I'm pretty sure she's harmless."

I shrugged and took back my notes, my cheeks heating like the top of a stove. "Maybe so. See you later."

Geez, that man got under my skin. What was God thinking when he made him drop-dead

41

gorgeous, with a teasing streak a mile long? No wonder Matt was single. He'd drive a woman bonkers within a day.

I slowed when I approached the house next to mine. Pastel yellow siding with blue trim made the house resemble an Easter egg. While many of the other neighbors worked in their yards on a sunny Saturday morning, no one puttered on the lawn of this house, or mine come to think of it. Low murmurs drifted from the back yard. Should I ring the doorbell, or knock on the gate? I opted for the door. Maybe they wouldn't answer. Westminster chimes played at the push of a button.

After several minutes, and two pushes later, I turned and surveyed the yard. I'd bet my sister that my neighbors hid in their backyard to avoid me. A rustling in the juniper bushes drew me that way. I advanced, holding my clipboard like a weapon.

When I approached within two feet, the bushes parted like the Red Sea and a man's face appeared. If not for the vacant look in his blue eyes, I might've called him handsome. Almost. Instead, a crew cut covered the top of a round head. One eye drifted to the right while the other lid looked ready to close. I couldn't tell whether he focused on me or not. When massive shoulders followed the head, I took a step back, suddenly aware of how flimsy of protection my clipboard would be.

"Hi." The man said.

"Hello. Do you live here?" I raised my makeshift weapon.

"No." He frowned. "Sometimes I forget where I live. I'm Rusty, I'm looking for someone."

"Who are you looking for?" He appeared harmless enough, so I lowered my arms. "Do you know the Edgarses?"

He shook his head. "Old Mrs. Lincoln got hurt. Bad." His eyes widened in owlish circles. The backyard gate creaked. He gasped, and the bushes closed around him.

What a strange man.

A man and woman straight out of a bad mob movie marched toward me. The woman's leopard-print, stiletto heels, which perfectly matched her leggings, sank into the yard with each step. Her bird's nest hairdo caused her to tower over the man next to her by several inches. Her husband, as tall and bulky as she was curvy, sported slicked back, inky hair and a goatee. My lips twitched in an effort to control my smile. They'd seen *Married to the Mob* one too many times.

"Good morning. I'm your nearest neighbor, Stormi Nelson."

"Cecelia Edgars." Her scarlet lips stretched into a smile. "We've seen you over the fence. Nice to finally meet you. This is my husband, Herman."

I nodded. "I'm checking on everyone, addressing concerns, after the murder of Mrs. Lincoln."

Herman stroked the hair on his chin and studied me with dark eyes. "That's very considerate of you. We do have a concern. We appear to have a peeping Tom."

Rusty would be the peeper, I'd guess. After my initial shock, he seemed harmless enough. "Should you call the police?"

Cecelia sunk blood red talons into her husband's forearm. "No, probably just some kid. Herman has a tendency to over-react sometimes."

I nodded. "Happens to the best of us. Would either of you like to join the Neighborhood Watch program?"

"No," Herman said. "We're way too busy." He turned, motioned for Cecelia to follow, then shoved open the gate.

"Nice meeting you," I called. Neither of them looked back.

A glance at my watch and a rumbling stomach, told me it was lunch time. I shuffled home, jotting notes next to the names.

"How'd it go?" Mom slapped a plate with a ham sandwich and a handful of chips in front of me. "Did you find some needy people to give food to?"

"No, I forgot to ask about food." Rusty might count as needy. I'd have to find out where he lived. "I did meet Matt's sister though. We're about the same age." I glanced around the quiet house. "Where is everyone?"

"Angela took the kids clothes shopping. They need things to wear for the summer." Mom plopped into the chair opposite me. "It sure will be nice to have a couple hours of quiet. They make a lot of noise."

I shrugged. Other than dirty dishes in the sink, and the occasional thundering up the stairs, I didn't know they were here. The two of them hid in their rooms with video games or the telephone.

"Let me see what you found out." Mom grabbed the clipboard. "Hmmm, very descriptive notes. I especially like the ones about the couple next door, and this Rusty person." She wrote 'Nelson and Nelson' on the top of the paper. "I'm going to be your sidekick. The Nelson Gumshoes. What do you think?"

I thought I was going to be sick. If she got involved, I'd never get the book written. "I'm only taking notes for a book, Mom. Not starting a new career."

"Doesn't matter. I'm good at this kind of stuff. I could do it with my eyes closed. It's been a long time since we were involved in something fun together."

My mother thought solving a murder was fun?

She tapped a fingernail on the paper. "Rusty killed the woman."

I almost choked on my sandwich. "Why do you say that?"

"I've caught him snooping around the place. No honest person does that." She crossed her arms. "If he wants to get to know us, all he has to do is ring the doorbell or yell 'howdy'. The man hasn't done anything but stare. Gives me the creeps."

"He can't help it." I wiped my mouth with a nearby napkin then reached for a glass of iced tea. "Besides, I don't have enough clues to make a guess yet."

"What do you need? Another dead body?"

6

I spewed soda across the table. Wiping my mouth with the back of my hand, I glared at Mom. "That's not funny."

"I'm perfectly serious. Another body would most likely give us clues. Don't you watch *Castle*, or *Criminal Minds*? They always shake things up with another murder. Even the best mystery authors use that trick. I should know more about it than you, considering I read more mysteries than anything else." Mom used a handful of napkins to dab at the dribble on my chin. "You really should watch them if you're going to write mysteries. You'll learn all kinds of tips."

Who was this woman and where was my mother? I moved her hand away from my chin and started cleaning up the drips on the table. Did I want a sidekick, much less for that sidekick to be my mother? The only reason I wanted to dig into Mrs. Lincoln's death was to write my book. I never considered actually solving the crime. But, wouldn't that be cool?

"Do you really think we can find out who the killer is?" I tossed the napkins in the garbage. And how much danger would we put ourselves in doing so?

"Sure. Somebody will, might as well be us. Think of the publicity, Stormi." Mom waved her arms. "Local Author Solves Murder. You'll sell a million books."

The idea did appeal to me. With the royalties, I could buy a nice car and hire an assistant to take care of the mundane aspects of being a writer. Someone to set up book-signings and such, thus leaving me with more time to actually spend writing.

"But I'd have to get out more. I'm already stretching myself thin going door to door. Mom, I go to sleep emotionally exhausted every day."

She patted my hand. "Your father died two years ago. It's time for you to rejoin the world and stop complaining about it."

She was right. "Okay, we'll do this. But, it won't be easy." Now, I'd do more than just take notes. Now, I'd be searching for a cold-blooded killer. Or a hot-blooded one, I guess, depending on the motive. I shuddered. Mom and I had lost our minds.

"What's going on?" Angela meandered into the kitchen and grabbed a soda from the fridge. "Y'all look like you're up to something."

"Nothing, dear." Mom winked. "How'd the shopping go?"

"Fine, other than expensive." Angela narrowed her eyes. "You two definitely have something up your sleeve, and I'm fixin' to find out what."

"We're talking about my next book. That's all."

I patted Mom on the shoulder as I went by. That'd stop my sister from being nosey. I don't think she'd cracked a book since High School required reading.

I headed up the stairs behind Cherokee and Dakota who dragged overflowing bags behind them. If my sister could go to the mall and spend hundreds of dollars on name brand clothing, why couldn't she afford another place to live?

Dakota closed his bedroom door and blasted some type of music that sounded more like screaming than singing. Cherokee did the same with Hip-Hop tunes. The doors might muffle some of the sound, but they didn't come close to the silence I craved. I sighed and shut myself in my office. What had I said earlier about not knowing they were there?

The thudding of somebody's stereo bass vibrated through the walls. My heart kept time with the beat. I pulled out my own set of headphones and covered my ears, then pulled a clean pad of yellow lined paper from the desk drawer. I went through a lot of pads. I seemed to think better with a fresh one in front of me and nothing beat taking notes with paper and a pencil.

I grabbed a mechanical pencil and promptly stuck the eraser end in my mouth. Mrs. Lincoln was killed in the backyard with a pair of gardening shears. I giggled. All I needed was who-dun-it. As a child, I'd always kicked butt at the game of Clue.

I had yet to meet a neighbor who liked the victim. Of course, I still had the other half of the neighborhood, but somehow I doubted I'd have any more success over there. On a positive note, I'd made a new friend and had the beginnings of a crush on a handsome detective. Neither of which would help me solve this thing. Maybe I did need my mother. She had a way of looking at things that others didn't, and my brain seemed to have frozen.

Sadie pawed at the door. I got out of my chair and let her in. "Do you want to go for a walk?" Maybe the fresh air would clear my head and let me think. Besides, I owned a dog now. For me to be a responsible owner Sadie would need regular walks. Walks that took me past a particular detective's house. I grinned and snapped my fingers for Sadie to follow me downstairs. Maybe having a dog would be the first step toward healing after my daddy's murder.

Once I'd hooked her leash to her collar, I skipped out the door and turned in the direction of Matt's house. Shirtless, tanned, muscular chest glistening with a light film of perspiration, he held a lawn blower and blew mowed grass and small twigs into a pile. I spotted a tattoo of a Celtic cross on his arm. If the man was any sexier, he'd be outlawed. I froze on the sidewalk and gaped like a fish.

It isn't like I hadn't seen a shirtless man before. For Pete's sake, I wrote about them. In great detail, I might add. But the sight of this particular one stole my breath and turned my limbs to jelly.

He caught sight of me, turned off the blower, and raised a hand. "Hey."

"Hey," I sounded like a frog with a cold. I tried again more clearly. "Hey, yourself."

Matt's long legs ate up the few yards between us. "Do you want to go to dinner with me Friday night?"

Wow. Uh. I chewed my pinkie nail. Dinner. In public. With a man I met three days ago.

"Sorry, but I'm afraid if I don't just blurt it out, I won't get up the nerve to ask." He grinned, dimples winking at me.

I wasn't expecting that and an acceptance blurted from me like a hole in a dam. I'd choke back my fear and try to enjoy myself. "I'd love to. Did you have anything planned, or would you rather I cooked for you?" No, that wouldn't work. Not unless he wanted to spend the evening with my flirty sister and loose-lipped mother, not to mention a couple of sullen teenagers.

I must've had some kind of strange look on my face because he laughed. "No, I'll take you somewhere nice. Wear something pretty. I'll pick you up at seven."

I grinned, doubting my feet touched the sidewalk as I continued Sadie's walk.

Something rustled in the bushes to my right. I stopped and squinted. My heart stopped at the sight of a pair of blue eyes, then calmed when I recognized Rusty. Didn't he have anything more pressing to do than spy on me and my dog? It creeped me out.

Besides, today the sun shone brighter, the sky bluer, the air fresher. All was right with my world since I accepted Matt's invitation. Funny. I haven't wanted to hide in my office all day, which didn't bode well for my writing career. Add in the fact that I didn't know how to garner more notes for my mystery story, and I found myself at a complete standstill. So, I might as well enjoy the company of a handsome man.

I increased my pace at the sight of Marion Henley's house. Maybe she wouldn't notice me. Sadie let out a solitary bark. Traitor.

"Hello, Stormi." Marion waved from where she knelt over a bent sprinkler head. "Find out any more about poor Ethel?"

"No. Why?"

"With all your nosiness, I thought you might've found out something."

"Who told you I was asking around?"

"I figured that out for myself." She stood and peeled pink-flowered gardening gloves from her hands. "I'm in my yard just about every day, and I saw you going door-to-door." She narrowed her eyes at me. "In my opinion, you need to be careful. No telling what might happen." With those encouraging words, she turned and marched into her house.

I tugged at Sadie's leash and quickened my pace. The sooner I got home, the sooner I could figure out what to wear to dinner. Something pretty, Matt had said. Other than my casual clothes and suits I wore to book-signings, pretty clothes didn't exist in my closet. Maybe Angela would lend me something that didn't let all my parts hang out and make me look like I ought to be loitering on a street corner.

Slamming the door, I headed up the stairs, yelling my sister's name.

Angela yanked her door open. "What?"

"I have a date on Friday." I bent to unclip

Sadie's leash from her collar.

"Repeat that." Angela tilted her head. Her forehead crinkled. "You have a date. You. Miss 'Stay to Herself in Front of the Computer and Type.'"

"Very funny." I brushed past her. "I don't have a thing to wear."

"That doesn't surprise me." She pointed to the bed. "Sit." Crossing her arms, she studied my face. "Do you need to wear those glasses?"

"If I want to see." What was wrong with them? I spent a lot of money on the flashy, black-rimmed, rhinestone-encrusted frames. "Besides, they make me look smart."

"You don't want to look smart on a date." Angela shoved open her closet. "Is this with Matt?"

"Yes. So keep it respectable."

"Sexy."

"Respectable." Maybe I should've found something to wear on my own.

"Hmmm." Angela tapped her finger against her lip and studied her clothes. "You aren't bad looking. And you can't get that shade of red on your head from a bottle, but I'm afraid your blue eyes get lost with those frames. What happened to your contacts?"

"They're in the bathroom. If I wear them, Matt will think I'm trying too hard. I want to look good, not desperate."

"But you are desperate. Or at least I would be if I lived your life."

"What are y'all doing?" Mom stepped into the room.

"Trying to make Stormi look pretty." Angela slid clothes aside, their hangers clanking against each other.

Try to make me look pretty? I removed the ties holding back my hair and shook it free so I could study the ends. Straight as a pencil. But wasn't that the style?

"She won't get rid of the glasses, Mom." Angela glared over her shoulder. "So I'll have to make do with artfully applied makeup and a gorgeous dress. Too bad her front side isn't bigger. You'd think with the money she makes, she would've taken care of that little problem."

"Forget it." I leaped up. "I'll do this myself."

Mom pointed at me. "Sit back down. We'll fix this. There's nothing a good bra can't improve."

I sat and crossed my arms. This was a bad idea.

"Here we go." Angela pulled out a black dress. "Go try this on."

I sighed, took the offered item of clothing, and shuffled to the bathroom. I knew, with all certainty, the dress would be inappropriate in some way. The dress belonged to Angela, after all. Friday was four days away. I had plenty of time to go shopping.

After discarding my daytime attire, I slipped into the dress and stood in front of the full length mirror. Wow. The dress fit me like a glove, emphasizing the curves I did have and shaping the ones God had skimped on. My hair glowed like fire against the fabric. Angela was right. The glasses had to go.

"Now, that," Angela said joining me, "is what a romance writer should wear. All your parts covered

53

up but looking hotter than asphalt during a heat wave. And you thought I only had slutty clothes."

I shrugged. What would she expect me to think when that's all I ever saw her wear? Lord, forgive me, but my sister wasn't even a smidgeon close to being Mother Theresa.

"You can keep the dress." She winked. "I've never worn it."

I laughed. "Thanks. I love it." Maybe I did need to update my wardrobe with things other than jeans and capris. I spotted the bags lying at the foot of my sister's bed. "Why so many new clothes?"

"I got a job." She grinned. "I'm the new receptionist at the police station."

7

With eyes gritty from contacts I rarely wore and my face painted to look like a movie star, I stared into the foyer mirror on Friday evening and wondered who the heck the woman looking back was. This woman didn't look afraid of life or too terrified to leave her community. Even I had to admit I cleaned up *gooood*. The doorbell rang. I smoothed my hair, and then rushed to answer it.

"No, you don't." Angela pushed me back. "A lady makes the man wait."

"Who made up that silly rule?"

"Everybody knows that." She pointed up the stairs. "Go to your room and wait fifteen minutes, at least."

"But Matt's here already." I moved toward the door again.

"No, Stormi. You don't want to appear too eager." Angela jabbed her finger in the air in the direction of the upper floor. "Go."

"Good grief, this is ridiculous." I stomped up the stairs feeling like a sixteen-year-old going on a first date. When Cherokee poked her head into the hall, I told her to shut up and go to her room. She laughed and closed her door, clearly pleased to see someone else at the end of her mother's bossy tongue.

I waited the allotted fifteen minutes then headed downstairs. With one hand on the hand rail, and the other propped flirtatiously on my hip, I tried to appear glamorous.

The heel of the ridiculous stiletto's my sister insisted I wear caught on the carpet runner. I grabbed the banister and bumped my way down to the foyer. Matt rushed to my side. Angela rolled her eyes and marched to the kitchen, muttering something under her breath about klutzy sisters.

"Are you all right?" Matt helped me up. His gaze, as slow and sure as his smile, traveled from my shoes to my hair. "You look amazing."

The smoldering look in his eyes almost made me forget my tumble and the bruises I'd sport tomorrow. His hand slid around my waist, making goose bumps trip across my skin. A tantalizing cologne of something woodsy and musk teased my senses. A slow smile lit up his face and stole my breath. I was doubly glad I'd finally made time to go down to the station and let an officer fill out that report. Now, if Matt asked, I wouldn't have to see disappointment cloud his eyes.

"You were worth waiting for." He handed me the black clutch from the foyer table then held open the front door. I waltzed through and glanced over my shoulder to the sight of my mother and sister peeking through parted kitchen curtains. Mom gave me a thumbs up.

In the driveway sat a black Hummer. How in the

world would I climb inside wearing this dress? One false move and I'd be showing parts of my wardrobe best left covered. Definitely something that would send me into an abyss of embarrassment. Matt must've noticed my look of alarm because before I knew it, the vehicle door was open, and I was swept into his arms and deposited on the passenger front seat. He winked and jogged to the driver's side.

I inwardly groaned and fought to refrain from burying my face in my hands. One mishap after another and we hadn't reached the restaurant yet.

Matt reached over and tucked my hair behind my ear, letting a few strands drape across his fingers. "Like silky fire. Beautiful enough to burn."

Could I melt any further? Where had this man been all my life? What if I said something stupid at dinner to run him off? In order to look anywhere but at him so he couldn't read my face, I stared out the window.

My eye caught sight of my overgrown lawn. Hiring a landscaper would be first on my to-do list for the morning before neighbors complained. I'd never lived anywhere folks cared so much about their yards.

"Have you ever been to Swank's Bistro?" Matt started the engine, then backed the truck from the driveway.

"We're going to Swank's?" Wow. Best, and most expensive, place in town. I didn't think cops made that kind of money. Oh. Maybe he was splurging for our date. I straightened. "No, I've never been there, but I've heard great things about it."

"I'm glad I'm the first to take you there."

Oh, he'd be the first to take me to a lot of places. Gracious. The hero in my next novel would definitely be modeled after Detective Steele. Stores wouldn't be able to keep copies on the shelf.

Fifteen minutes later, we pulled into the parking lot of the restaurant and were seated in front of a large plate glass window as the sun began to set. Magenta and lavender rays spilled across the crisp white tablecloth in front of us. A gas lamp burned low. Muted murmurs of other guests reached my ears. Soft music played in the background. I decided right then and there I was going to marry Matthew Steele, and he'd propose to me in this very spot.

"What are you thinking about? You look a million miles away." Matt smiled before greeting the waitress. He ordered a bottle of red wine and turned his attention back to me.

My cheeks flamed. "Oh, uh. The lake and fountain outside are gorgeous."

"So is the view across the table." He lifted his menu and peered over its edge. "Do you see anything you like?"

Did I? Oh, on the menu. I glanced at the glossy pages, settling on filet mignon with blue-cheese crust.

The waitress arrived again, poured our wine, took our order, then silently left. Matt lifted his glass. "To the first of many such nights."

I grinned like a silly love-struck girl and lifted my glass in return. "Thank you for inviting me." By the time our meal came, the sun had set fully, casting us into a romantic dusk. I lifted my knife and fork, noting how much tonight resembled a scene from one of my novels. Would it end in a kiss as the scene had? I needed to divert my thoughts, quickly. After all, there was still the small chance that Matt was a dirty cop. No one could be scratched off my suspect list.

"How's the case coming?"

"Which one?" Matt cut a piece of steak and lifted his fork.

"Mrs. Lincoln. I've decided to continue investigating to gather clues for my book. My mother is going to help. So far—"

"Hold up." A muscle twitched in his jaw, and his hand tightened around his fork. "I thought I asked you to stay out of it."

"Well," I buttered a slice of bread. "I was going to, but realized how exciting solving a crime might be, not to mention the publicity, Mom's idea, for my next book. And I have this phobia, that I'm hoping… well, it's a miracle really that I'm sitting here with…"

With precision, Matt set his utensils on each side of his plate. "Mrs. Lincoln was killed violently. We found defensive wounds on her hands and arms. We figure she must've turned to run before being stabbed in the back." He speared me with his gaze. "Is this really what you want to get messed up in? Put yourself in the same kind of danger, not to mention the possible danger to your family?"

"I hadn't thought of it that way." The blood rushed to my feet. My head swam. I could see the sense in what he said, but having him practically forbid me to snoop around, didn't sit well with me.

"Am I breaking the law?" I sat back and crossed my arms.

"Not yet." Matt mimicked my body language. "Have you been back to the crime scene?"

I shook my head. "There's nothing left to see there." My eyes widened." Unless … did Mrs. Lincoln have a storage shed full of gardening equipment? Was she killed with her own shears, or someone else's?"

Matt leaned his elbows on the table and fixed his gaze, unblinking, on my face. "Did you accept my invitation to dinner so you could grill me about the case?"

"No." I turned away from the pain on his face and stared out the window. I wasn't a good conversationalist. Talking about the death of Mrs. Lincoln seemed like a good idea at the time. A topic of conversation we were both interested in. Obviously, I'd been wrong. I faced him. "I accepted your invitation because I like you. You're cute."

"Cute?" His mouth twitched. "Are we in Junior High? What about devastatingly handsome?"

I giggled, relieved he'd chosen to see through my stupid attempt at conversation, and held onto the offered olive branch with both hands. "Don't be too sure of yourself, Detective."

"I'm quite confident in my ability to woo women." He resumed eating.

Thank you, God. I'd almost blown a perfectly good evening. I chewed a mouthful of tender steak. Obviously, any clue gathering I accomplished would have to be done without Detective Steele.

It wasn't like I planned on making a career out of solving crime. I just wanted to gather enough information to write a stellar book. A few pages of notes, and I could go back to closing myself behind my office door and putting fingers to the keyboard.

I turned my brightest smile on Matt and lifted my glass in a toast. "To the cutest boy in the restaurant."

He laughed. "And to the prettiest girl."

I could do this. Enjoy a flirtatious relationship with Matt, and snoop when he wasn't around. The key would be to watch my tongue. Things could get tricky with him being an officer of the law. I peered at him over the top of my wineglass and wished I lived alone again so I could invite him in for a romantic movie and popcorn. Maybe we could prolong the evening with a walk around the neighborhood.

"Can I tempt y'all with dessert?" The waitress stood beside the table, a shortened pencil poised over her pad.

"Not for me, thank you." I smiled.

"Me either. Just the check." Matt leaned across the table. "Want to come back to my place?"

I choked, wine dribbling down my chin. Had he read my mind? I might think those types of things, write about them, but ran the opposite direction as fast as possible when approached. Years of Mom's lectures about what good girls did and didn't do, still ricocheted in my head like a ping-pong ball.

"I, uh, thought maybe we could take a walk?"

He chuckled. "If that's what you want."

My heart stopped trying to beat free, and I

occupied myself by dabbing at the white tablecloth and ground the wine deeper into the fabric. I was thankful for the dim lighting because my face probably burned brighter than the noonday sun.

Matt placed a hand over mine. "Relax, Stormi. I won't do anything but give you a goodnight kiss and my phone number."

Mercy.

8

"Why are all the lights off?" Matt pulled into the driveway. "You should at least leave your porch light on for security purposes."

"Mom always goes to bed early. Most likely Angela did, too. She's excited about starting her job on Monday. It does seem strange to me that she'll be working at the station. She isn't that reliable, but that's y'all's problem now. The kids are probably out with friends." *Quit babbling, Stormi. You'll run the guy off before you know what it's like to kiss him.*

Matt cut the ignition and turned in his seat. The moon cast him into shadow. He crooked a finger. "Come here."

Oh, Mama. My heart beat so fast I thought my chest would explode. He's going to kiss me. Did I have garlic for dinner? Blue cheese. Oh, no.

I shook my head. "Mom will kill me if she looks out and we're kissing in the car in front of the neighbors like a couple of teenagers." Although it might be fun, I wasn't taking any chances of kissing him with cheese breath. I needed a diversion.

He chuckled. "You're right. Let's wait until we

get to the front door."

I needed to do something about my breath. Now. I had gum in my purse. After I shifted my legs, my purse fell and spilled on the floor. While hiding behind my hair, I scrounged for a stick of gum and crammed it in my mouth. I'd spit it in the bushes when we approached the porch. I scooped the few remaining items into my clutch and straightened. "Ready." Not really, but anticipation was building like a shaken soda bottle.

With his hand warm on my lower back and my nerves strung as tight as my dress, Matt led me to the front door. As if he handled a new born baby, he turned me to face him. I raised my face and swallowed my gum.

With delicious slowness, he kissed my forehead, each cheek, my nose, then laid a tender kiss on my lips. "Goodnight." He chuckled and jogged to his Humvee.

Thank goodness the door was there to hold me up, because no way could my legs do the job. Plus, there was a full-scale jazz band playing in my stomach and the nerves that were strung tight now tingled. I released my pent-up breath in a shaky sigh. Just like the hero of a best-selling author, Matt's kiss left me wanting more. I reached behind me, opened the door, and froze.

Wait. I didn't care what I'd told Matt. A dark house. An unlocked door. It all spelled trouble. "Sadie? Ebony? Ivory?" Where were my pets? My family?

I grabbed a heavy crystal candlestick off the foyer table as my weapon and slid against the wall and toward the dining room. Like one of Charlie's Angels, I jumped around the wall, legs shoulder-width apart, candle holder held like a nine-millimeter. Nothing. I kicked off my shoes and moved into the kitchen. Black and white paws poked from under the pantry door. Sad meowing echoed from within the tiny closet of a space. My babies!

After setting them free, I scooped them into my arms and nuzzled them against my neck. My gaze fell on the short counter beside the refrigerator. Where was my clipboard?

Clutching the cats, who by this time were beginning to squirm against my tight grip, I thudded up the stairs and into my bedroom. I tossed the cats on the bed and locked the door. Why would somebody want my clipboard? And I still hadn't located Sadie. Tears welled in my eyes at the thought that she might've ran off. I dug through my purse for Matt's phone number and punched it into my cell phone.

"Matt?"

"Stormi? Why are you whispering?"

"Somebody broke into my house and locked up my cats." The poor things. They were so traumatized all they could do was groom themselves. "I can't find my dog." Oh. No one told me whether I could keep Sadie or not. Maybe a family member of Mrs. Lincoln's saw her in the yard and took her. A sob escaped me.

"Are you sure somebody broke in?"

"My clipboard is missing, and the cats were locked in the pantry." I snatched a tissue from my nightstand. "I kept the clipboard beside the refrigerator." I lowered my voice further. "The front door was unlocked."

"What about other rooms in the house?"

"I locked myself in my room. But I can check my office." I shuffled across the room and flicked on the light in my office. Desk drawers were pulled out. Books were tossed on the floor. "It's ransacked." The one sure place I felt safe at any time had been violated, taken from me.

I sagged against the wall. Where could I go for peace now? Where could I ever feel safe after tonight?

"Hang up and call the police." Click.

Matt *was* the police. I didn't want anyone else to see me like this. I didn't want *him* to see me with puffy eyes and a red nose. I rushed back to the bed and scooted against the headboard before gathering pillows around me. I'd settle in and wait for rescue while my breathing regulated and my heartbeat returned to normal.

I prayed that Mom and the others really did go somewhere tonight. Maybe they even took Sadie with them. Or … what if they were dead and buried in the backyard? What would I do? I'd have to sell the house. No way could I continue to live here. No, surely somebody would've heard something. You couldn't kill four people and not make a sound. As bothersome as my family tended to be at times, I didn't want any harm to come to them. I loved them.

A floorboard creaked outside my door. The knob turned. My fingers poised over the buttons on my phone.

Ebony and Ivory yowled and skittered under the bed.

My mouth turned into the Sahara desert. I might not have been much of a praying person lately, but petitions for safety flew to heaven faster than food disappeared from a buffet line at a fat camp.

The footsteps moved away. Moments later, a shadow appeared in the doorway between my room and my bathroom. I gripped one of the pillows, took aim, and let it fly.

"What the …?" Matt flicked on the light. "Was that supposed to stop an intruder?"

"It's all I had available. I left the candlestick in the kitchen." I slid from the bed and launched myself into his arms. Sobs overtook me. "How did you get in? I locked the door."

"You only locked your bedroom." He held me at arm's length. "Are you okay?"

I nodded, and sniffed.

"Good. Lock all the doors to your room. I'm going to take a look around." He pulled his weapon from a holster under his arm. "Backup should be here soon."

"I didn't call them."

He set his jaw. "Why not?" He managed to grind out.

"You are the cops. I was all ready to call, though, then you showed up. I want to come with you."

"No."

I crossed my arms. "I'll come anyway. You might as well give in."

He ran a hand through his hair. "Stay behind me. I can't believe I'm doing this."

I placed a hand on each of his shoulders and allowed him to lead me from dark room to dark room. When we'd finished, he turned on the kitchen light and pulled his cell phone from his pocket. He pointed at the table for me to sit then punched numbers into his phone. After placing a call for officers to investigate my house in more detail, Matt pulled out a chair, flipped it around, and straddled it, his gaze locked on my face.

After several seconds, I smoothed my hair. "What? Do I have something on my face?"

He shook his head. "No. We haven't known each other long, but I have a strong suspicion that you're one of those people who manage to find trouble without looking."

"No, I'm not, at least not until I decided to write mysteries. Then everything changed."

"Didn't you say you decided to change your genre after you tripped over Mrs. Lincoln's body?"

Did the man never blink? And he had the memory of an elephant.

The front doorknob rattled. Matt had his hand on his gun, stood, and yanked me behind him before the sound fully registered. Mom, followed closely by Sadie, strolled into the kitchen.

"I thought you two had a date." She patted Sadie's head as the dog rushed to my side.

I knelt and buried my face in her fur. "I thought I'd lost you, you silly mutt."

"The dog needed a walk. So did I." Mom opened the refrigerator, pulled out a soda, then sat at the table. "And you of all people know it isn't safe to walk outside alone, especially at night. Look what happened less than a week ago. Now, if you were doing your job as head of the Neighborhood Watch properly … well, it might be different around here." She peered at me for a moment, then cocked her head.

"Are you all right, sweetie?"

"I'm fine, Mom." I laid my still trembling hands flat on the table top.

"Because I know how you are about leaving your house, and—"

"I'm getting better." Please drop the subject. I didn't want Matt to know what a wimp I was. Only Mom knew how hard it was for me to take on the role of head of the Neighborhood Watch. But I'd gone out a few times now and still walked among the living.

Matt sighed. "Mrs. Nelson, someone broke into your home tonight. Please try not to touch anything."

"What'd they take?" She glanced around the room. "Not much of value around here."

"The notes I took on the case." I crossed my arms.

"No, they didn't. I stuck those in that drawer by the sink. We can't have stuff cluttering the counters."

Matt pulled out the drawer. Sure enough, neon pink shined up at us.

I crossed my arms. "Okay, then. Did you mess up my office?"

She waved her hand. "It's always messy."

"Not like it is now." I have never left my work space is such disarray. How dare she tease like that?

"Ladies, please." Matt pinched the bridge of his nose.

Red and blue lights flashed outside the window. Matt looked so relieved, I thought he'd knock the door down getting outside. Five minutes later, he returned with two other officers and led them upstairs.

I slouched in my chair, knowing he wouldn't welcome my company during official business. He'd labeled me as a troublemaker. Not even his kiss was good enough to make me forget a remark like that one.

Oh, who was I kidding? His kisses could make me forget anything.

With a sigh, I propped my chin in my hand and stared out the kitchen door. Footsteps thumped upstairs. I should be up there taking notes. I shifted my gaze to Mom. "Where's Angela and the kids?"

Mom waved a dismissive hand. "Parent night at the school or something. Good thing we weren't here. We could've been killed. You really need to get people to sign up for the Watch, unless you plan on doing it yourself every night."

"I don't. Will you join?"

"Guess I already did since I took a stroll tonight. Kept my eyes peeled, too. Everything's quiet." She took another sip of her soda. "You might want to hire a gardener, though. Our house is the most ill-kept in the neighborhood, except for Mrs. Lincoln's. Seems she didn't take too good of care of hers either. It's embarrassing."

"I noticed myself. I'll call tomorrow." I jumped to my feet as Matt and another officer marched into the room.

"We need you to take a look and see if anything is missing." Matt narrowed his eyes. "But don't touch anything."

The moment I stepped into my office I noticed my laptop was on. "Somebody was on my computer. I always turn the monitor off when I'm done."

"What were you working on?" Matt had donned gloves at some point and he moved the mouse to bring the screen to life.

"My mystery."

"Why would someone care about that?"

"Excuse me?" My face heated. "People happen to like my novels."

"That's not what I meant. Why would someone break into your house to read a story that isn't complete?"

I shrugged. "Oh. It's the story I'm writing off the notes I've been taking." I gasped. "The neighborhood killer was in my house."

"We don't know that." Matt straightened and gave me a stern look. "Don't start assuming things."

Crime scene investigators arrived, and he motioned for them to dust the computer. Great. How long until I could use it again?

"That's my guess, too." Mom stepped into the room. "Stormi knows something she shouldn't and someone is out to silence her." In her hands, she held a bowl of popcorn. As she shoved a handful in her mouth, kernels fell to the floor.

"Mrs. Nelson, please. You're contaminating the scene." Matt took her by the elbow and moved her into the hall. His silent partner stared, pencil poised over a small spiral notebook.

"Don't worry. You'll get used to the craziness if you're here long enough." I turned and returned to the kitchen. Too late for soda or coffee. Maybe a glass of juice would quench my thirst. I opened the refrigerator.

I grabbed the orange juice and squinted. Where was my raspberry tea? If Cherokee or Dakota got into my stuff, there would be a high price to pay. I poured juice into a glass and replaced the carton. Wait. What if the thief stole my drink? It'd been known to happen. I saw on television all the time where crooks sat down to eat and drink after their crime.

"Mom!"

"Yes, dear." She placed the bowl of popcorn on the table.

"Where's my tea? Do you think the kids drank it?"

She shook her head. "They tried it once and didn't like it. Or so they said."

"You're missing something?" Matt leaned against the doorframe.

Should I really let him know how much I liked my drink? I closed the fridge. "Nope."

"Her tea is gone. She's the only one who touches the stuff. I prefer wine myself," Mom volunteered. "Angela is into harder stuff, unfortunately. Or beer." She grimaced. "I don't know where I went wrong with that girl."

"Does she make a habit of leaving her cans around?" That would explain Sadie the drunk.

"No, she tries to hide that she drinks, but a mother always knows."

Matt sighed and glanced at me. "We're finished. Walk me to the door?"

Would I? "I really enjoyed our date, Matt. Sorry you had to come over here again."

He gave me that lopsided grin that caused my heart to stop. "I'm not sorry." He caressed my cheek. "Call me any time. Please, be careful." Again, he left me weak against the door post with a kiss to the temple.

"I need to rethink getting involved in this mystery," I told Mom as I closed the door.

"No, you need to stay in it. Somebody seems to think you know more than you do. You're a target now."

9

The next night, I donned a pair of jogging shorts and slipped into my comfiest sneakers before motioning Sadie to follow me into the hall. Since I still hadn't made time to set up another Neighborhood meeting, the Watch still consisted of one member—me. Oh, two.

Mom came out of her room in a black jogging suit. One of Dakota's dark knit beanies stretched as low over her face as she could pull it and still see. She took one look at me and her mouth fell open. "How can we set up a sting operation if you're wearing colors that glow in the dark?"

Smoothing my canary yellow tee-shirt, I frowned. "Sting operation?"

"We're going on the Watch walk, right? I thought we could stop by the dead lady's house and look for clues."

I thought about explaining the difference between snooping and a sting, but gave it up as a waste of time. "The lady's name is, was, Ethel Lincoln, and we can't go snooping around place. It's a crime scene, and we can go to jail. There's no reason for me to change my clothes.

We're going to walk the neighborhood and make sure everything is peaceful. That's all."

"Suit yourself, but they took the tape down this morning." Mom grinned. "I have it all planned. We take Sadie to the yard and let her go. She'll waltz right into her old home. We'll have to fetch her, of course. Can't leave the poor thing all alone." She snapped rubber gloves over her hands, then grabbed a flashlight from the foyer table. "Ready?"

Not really, but I led the way out the front door anyway, and glanced toward Matt's house. His truck was gone. Good. I didn't relish being hauled to jail, not even if the detective looked like a magazine cover model. Of course, if I got to share a cell with him, it might be worth it. Knowing my luck, it'd be a three-hundred-pound woman named Bertha˙ looking for a "friend". I shuddered. "I already tried this plan, and it didn't work."

Mom might look like she wanted to remain incognito, but she waved at every man, woman, and child we passed. We garnered quite a few odd looks, too. Maybe the skip in Mom's step aroused interest. Either way, I felt as if I were walking a first grader to class. Before we reached the late Mrs. Lincoln's house, sweat stained Mom's shirt and trickled down her face. Giggles overtook me.

"It's not funny." Mom yanked the beanie off her head, leaving her hair standing on end like someone who'd been electrocuted. "Who knew tonight would be like a sauna?"

Dakota skateboarded toward us, performed an Ollie, and came to a banging stop that echoed up and down the street. If not for his incessant talk about his hobby, I wouldn't have had a clue about his trick. As it was, I felt pretty proud of myself for remembering. "Nice Ollie."

He raised his eyebrows. "Yeah, thanks. What's up? Ain't this where the dead lady lived?"

"Yes, now get." Mom waved him toward home. "We're on official mystery business. Here take your beanie back."

I sighed. Nothing like piquing a kid's interest.

"Can I come?" He kicked his board up into his waiting hands and accepted his beanie.

"No, you can't." Mom gave him a little shove. "This is adult's only."

"Whatever." Dakota inserted the ear buds hanging around his neck, dropped the board with another clatter, then skated off.

"Mom, please don't tell everyone what we're doing. We don't need an audience." Especially since we were most likely breaking the law on many levels. I dragged her into the thick hedge surrounding Mrs. Lincoln's property. "If we're doing this, we have to be quiet."

"Okey doke." She bent and unhooked the leash from Sadie's collar. With a smack on the dog's rump, she announced, "Go get 'em, girl."

Sadie barked once and dashed into the night. Well, there was no turning back now. I'd have to fetch the dog. Matt was going to kill me. Wrap those big hands around my neck, shove my head back, and … I decided to stop before my thoughts turned in a direction that would keep me up at night.

I followed Mom to the back of the house. Weeds and knee-high grass filled the yard except for the packed dirt around the doghouse. I tried the door. Locked. An open window mocked us from two feet above our heads. "Well, that's that. No way in."

"Don't be silly." Mom put her hand on my shoulder. "Give me a boost. Once I'm in, I'll open the kitchen door."

"Not a good idea. The window's only open about six inches, give or take. Maybe I should go first." Against my better judgment, of course.

"Stop being such a sissy. I might weigh twenty pounds more than you, but I'm not an obese cow by any means. My curves are in all the right places. You can ask any man that likes his woman soft. Now, do what I say."

I rolled my eyes, braced my shoulder against the siding of the house, and cupped my hands. How much jail time could a person get for breaking and entering? Was it considered breaking if a window was left open? My stomach churned and sweat broke out on my brow that had nothing to do with the warmer than normal spring evening.

Mom planted her foot in my hand and jumped. Ugh! I fell to the ground under her weight. She kicked and flailed, her bottom raised to the moon. She looked as stuck as a tightened pickle jar lid. I had the insane urge to whack her with the handle of a butter knife to loosen her.

"Help me," she hissed. "Push."

"How am I supposed to push you through a tiny opening from down here?" Seriously. Her legs kicked above my head and her butt jiggled as she tried to worm her way through.

"Just do it!"

I stared at the sky, wondering what I'd done to deserve this. Realizing someone could spot Mom's spandex-covered lower body, of which her leggings drooped dangerously low, I dragged over an empty bucket that most likely came from a home improvement store. After upending it and stepping up, I planted my shoulder under Mom. One, two, three, I shoved. Nothing. The bucket tottered. "I'm not tall enough."

"I swear I moved a smidgen. Do it again."

With a deep breath and a grunt, I heaved. Mom tumbled through the window.

The bucket beneath me overturned, and I fell to the grass. My hip slammed against a decorative boulder. Once Mom unlocked the door, I was going to strangle her. This little night time escapade had better not be a waste of time. It'd been days since I'd written a word on one of my novels, and adventures like this one left me unsure whether I actually wanted to write a mystery. It seemed too dangerous.

Hip throbbing, I struggled to my feet and leaned against the side-paneling of the house to wait for Mom. Through the skinny window beside the door, I caught glimpses of her flashlight. What was taking her so long? Five seconds. That's all it should've taken for her to unlock it. I pounded on the glass.

She whirled, catching me in the eye with the bright beam. "Be right there!" Her yell blasted through the open window.

I banged again and glanced over my shoulder. "Let me in before somebody sees me."

A squad car cruised down the street, and I shrank into the shadows of a tall oak tree. Come on, Mom. Visions of handcuffs and steel bars rippled through my mind. With Mom as my supposed sidekick, arrest was a breath away. I just knew it.

After an eternity, the lock clicked and the kitchen door swung open. I slid through like a greased monkey, slammed the door shut, and leaned against raised-paneled wood, willing my heart rate to slow its stampede. As my eyes adjusted to the dark room, I glanced around. The overgrown yard had nothing on the inside of Mrs. Lincoln's home.

A pine table lay buried under mounds of clothes and papers. Dishes, clean and dirty, covered every inch of the kitchen counter and filled the sink. A wooden knife block, full of dusty knives, was wedged between the wall and the microwave. The floor crunched under my feet. How in the world could a person find anything in this place? I shoved away from the door and pulled a tiny pin light out of my pocket. Scooting sideways, I moved down the hall after Mom's bobbing light.

I didn't expect to find anything. Not since the police had already canvassed the place, but there was always the chance they might've missed something. I ran the beam of light over the piles of magazines and shopping bags lining the hall. Taking care not to crush anything, I stepped into the room on my right. A bathroom so cluttered you couldn't pay me to use it. Not with an inch-thick layer of soap scum and hair across every surface.

Next, I came to what was clearly a home office.

I moved the mouse next to the computer. A

genealogy chart popped onto the screen. Interesting. I'd research my own roots someday. The important question now was, "Why hadn't the cops taken the computer?" I glanced at a padded bag on the floor. From what I could tell, they'd taken a laptop. Why not the desktop? Obviously they weren't interested in the facts of a woman tracing her roots.

The miniscule glass topped desk seemed out of place in the house. Out of place in the fact that except for the computer, phone, and a pad of legal sized paper, it was clear of mounds of stuff. I shined my light on the pad, noting the names of residents up and down my street. Two names were circled, Rusty and the Edgars. All the others had only a check. What did it mean? Was Mrs. Lincoln planning something? A party maybe? Where would she put her guests? On top of the mounds of garbage?

"Mom, did you find anything?" I turned back to the hall.

"There's a lot of new gardening tools in the master bedroom. That's weird." She poked her head into the hall then withdrew. I followed.

Tools covered the dresser and the bed. Scanning the room with my light, I counted two of everything, except for shears. Only one pair of red-handled shears lay on top of the dresser. Had Mrs. Lincoln been killed by one of her own tools?

Death and evil hovered in the air. Despair. A life cut short. Bile rose in my throat. "I'm ready to go now, please."

"But this woman had a lot of neat things." Mom's light moved closer. "Don't you want to look around more?"

"We can't snoop through a dead woman's house for no reason."

"Fine. But I don't think she'd care. Not at this point, anyway." She sighed and pushed past me. "Let's lock up and go back through the window."

Once Mom exited safely outside, I locked the door and followed, wiggling my way through. My legs dangled. "A little help here."

Strong hands grasped my waist, pulled me down, and I turned to stare at the solid wall of Matt's chest.

10

"What are you doing?" Matt set me on my feet and crossed his arms. I focused on the infamous tic in his jaw. Had he had it before meeting me?

"Uh. Looking for Sadie?" I glared at Mom who stood silently off to the side, a sheepish look on her face.

"This Sadie?" Matt unwound a leash from a lawn chair and handed the dog to me. "It would be a remarkable feat for her to climb through a six foot high window, don't you think?"

I took the leash. "She's a very smart dog and very big."

Frustration and disappointment stained his handsome features. He drew air roughly through his nose and shook his head. "Why won't you listen when I give you advice? You're going to force me to do something I don't want to do. Go. Home." He gave a chest-heaving sigh, about-faced and marched in the opposite direction.

I glared at Mom before turning toward home. My steps dragged. Matt probably wouldn't ask me to dinner again, nor allow me to be friends with his sister. He glanced over his shoulder. I'd blown any chance at being in his life. Maybe not.

I'd cook him something nice and drop it off tomorrow. That would soften him up. It worked in books and movies.

"If you would've worn all black, like me, this wouldn't have happened." Mom kicked a loose stone off the sidewalk. "But it sure was fun."

My mouth gaped. Most of the time, Mom didn't seem to have the sense God gave a goose, but I loved her to pieces, and even more, loved the fact we were actually hanging out together.

So, what did that say about me when I followed her hare-brained schemes like a little gosling? I laughed. But, I did have to admire her adventuring spirit. I threw my arm around her shoulders. "I love you, Mom, but you sure do beat all."

"I love you, too, sweetie." She flashed a brilliant smile. "Sorry about getting you into trouble with your man."

"He isn't my man." I wished he was, though. Wouldn't that be grand? Mrs. Matthew Steele. I'd change my author name to Stormi Steele. Oh, that sounded wonderful.

Someone shrieked; an angry sound ripping through the night. Then a cry — a mixture of pain, anger, and resignation all whipped together — followed by the deeper rumble of a man's voice.Sadie ducked behind me and whimpered.

Mom and I glanced at each other then dashed across the street, half-dragging my cowardly dog. I pointed to our right. "I think the noise came from there."

"Wait." Mom grabbed my arm. "Maybe we

should call the police."

"Probably a good idea, but I didn't bring my cell phone." When would I remember to stick it in my pocket when I left the house? "If somebody's in trouble, there isn't time to go home first." I yanked Sadie's leash. She dug her paws into the grass and hunched her shoulders. "Come on."

Another shriek echoed from behind one of the houses.

"Tie her to a tree and leave her." Mom moved to a jog.

I hated to leave behind my cowering friend, but I slipped the handle of her leash over a tree limb and sprinted after Mom. Careening around the corner of a pale-colored Victorian, I skidded to a stop in the alley and slipped on the loose gravel. My arms flailed like a windmill but I kept my footing and concentrated on the couple in front of me.

Behind a massive hydrangea bush partially covering a screened-in porch, the neighborhood's blond bombshell, Victoria, struggled with a man. He gripped her upper arms, shook her, and let loose a string of curse words strong enough to singe my eyebrows.

"I didn't. I swear." Tears rolled down Victoria's cheeks. "The simpleton stared through the window with no invitation from me. You know how he is, skulking around, watching people"

"Right. Like the time I caught you dancing in your underwear for Mr. Edgars." The man shoved her away from him.

"That was my job. I was at work." Victoria covered her face. "Besides, you know I don't dance for money anymore."

It's not that I wanted to eavesdrop or witness such a tragic scene, but I couldn't tear myself away. Mom didn't do any better. Like teenagers catching their first glimpse of an R-rated movie, we stared.

My life once existed in peaceful surroundings like a Norman Rockwell painting. At least until two years ago when Dad died from a wayward bullet between gang members. Then, just when I thought I might have things together again, all this happened. Violence of any sort had a tendency to unnerve me.

When the stranger noticed us and took a step in our direction, I took a step back. Please, don't hit me. I bruise easily.

"Who are you? What do you want?" He clenched his hands at his sides and continued to advance.

I straightened as tall as my five-foot-two inches would take me. "I'm head of the Neighborhood Watch."

He laughed; a cold humorless sound. Goosebumps raised on my arms. "Good for you."

Time for a bit of grits. "Mom, give me your flashlight." I held out my hand and wrapped my fingers around the hard plastic.

Like a scene from David and Goliath, the man towered over me. The streetlamp's glow stretched his shadow before us like a creature from the pit of hell. My stomach dropped. Surely David's knees had shook as mine did; his heart beat the same irregular tattoo.

Victoria sniffled behind the angry man and held out her hands, mumbling something sounding to me like, "Bob, it'll be all right, don't do anything rash," etc.

At least I had a name for the enraged man. But, Bob was about to get the shock of his life. I might be small, but I could pack a mighty wallop when scared. I raised the flashlight and whapped him on the head.

He cradled his head. "What the …?"

Victoria leapt to his aid, spitting, and screeching like a treed cat. "Why'd you hit him? He wasn't going to hurt you. Bob wouldn't hurt a fly."

The poor man groaned and slid to the ground. Really? That's right, big boy. Play it up, Superman. I could see the marks from his fingers forming on the pale skin of Victoria's upper arm. Why did she defend him? This is why I chose to stay home in my office and deal with imaginary people. They made more sense.

Footsteps pounded behind us. I thrust the flashlight at Mom as Matt barreled into our merry group. She dropped it. It spun in a circle, illuminating each of us in flashes of light, but the only face I focused on was the stern one of Matt. Disappointment twice in one night. Would our relationship ever recover?

"What's going on?" Matt crossed his arms.

"That woman," Bob pointed at me. "Smacked me in the head with a lethal weapon."

"It was a flashlight. A cheap one dollar flashlight from Wal-Mart." I rolled my eyes and mimicked Matt's posture. "Besides, he was hurting Victoria and making menacing advances toward me."

"Miss. Lanham?" Matt glanced at her.

"I'm fine." She gripped Bob's arm as he stood. "No harm done. These women interfered where they aren't wanted and attacked my boyfriend."

"Good grief." How could she be so dumb? Surprisingly, Mom kept her mouth shut. The one time I could've used her to side with me, and she chose to act like a clam, and left me looking like a hysterical bystander.

Matt moved to my side. "I'll walk you home."

"But—"

"If she doesn't want to press charges, there's nothing we can do." He leaned closer. A whiff of his cologne sent my stomach fluttering. "It'd be wise to leave before *he* decides to press charges against *you*."

I sputtered, but allowed him to lead me away. Mom followed like a docile puppy. We retrieved Sadie and continued home. After we reached my porch steps, Matt ushered Mom into the house and faced me.

"Can't you stay out of trouble for ten minutes?" He plopped onto the porch swing and patted the cushion beside him.

Although I wasn't in the mood for a lecture, I sat and let the swinging motion lull me to a sense of peace. "I don't go looking for it, Matt. I was walking home, like you told me to, and heard a woman scream."

"It didn't occur to you to call the police?"

"I didn't have my phone." I glanced at his strong profile. The urge to have him kiss me burned through my veins. My face heated, and I stared across the dark yard so he couldn't use the glow of the porch light to read the emotions on my face. "I couldn't ignore a cry for help."

"I'm not sure I can do this," he mumbled. He sighed deep enough to vibrate the wooden back of the swing. "Stormi, if you interfere in my investigation again, or put you or your mother in danger, I *will* arrest you."

"Interfere how?" I leaped to my feet. "I was walking home. How is that breaking the law?" Letting him know it was all Mom's idea might get him off my back a little, but, no. As an adult, I had the right to choose to follow my mother's crazy schemes without answering to a man.

Matt stood and leaned close enough I could see the moon cast sparks of light in his eyes, like daggers of cold fire. "You entered a crime scene without permission."

"The tape was gone." I planted my fists on my hips. By this time, our noses almost touched.

"It's private property!"

"My dog got loose."

"My guess is you let her loose." Matt grabbed fistfuls of his hair and turned away from me. "Ugh."

"I can't talk to you like this." Tears burned my eyes.

"The feeling's mutual." He stormed down the stairs and across the yard.

A sob tore at my throat. With everything in me, I willed him to turn around and run back to me. But this wasn't like one of my romance novels. He wasn't going to do what I wanted, willed or not. I didn't hold the pen to write this love story.

Matt halted at the sidewalk. His shoulders slumped. The sob lodged in my throat as I stared at his back. He whirled and sprinted up the walk. He took the steps two-at-a-time and halted in front of me.

"You drive me to distraction," he growled. He put his hands on each side of my face and stared into my eyes. "You're like a drug."

Then he kissed me; A hard, rough, kiss. The kind that claimed ownership and stated frustration. The lip smashed against teeth, bruising, blood-boiling kind of kiss.

I slipped my arms around his neck and held on, letting the turbulent storm carry me while I returned his passion with equal fervor. My legs weakened, and we fell backward onto the swing. The wood dug into my spine, and I squirmed, moaning. My fingers tangled in his hair. I didn't want the kiss to end, ever.

Matt broke contact and chuckled, his breathing heavy. "If you keep moving like that I can't be responsible for my actions."

"The swing's digging into my back." Wonderful. He must think I'm a tease.

He stood and offered his hand to pull me up. "And, here I thought it was my kisses." With a gentle tug, he pulled me against his chest and tilted my chin. "You frighten me more than anything I've ever encountered." He brushed his lips across mine and left me standing wobbly-legged as he loped down the road.

Mercy! I ought to bottle the man. I'd make a fortune.

Now, I needed to find a way to continue locating clues without losing what promised to be a blood-rushing relationship.

Something rustled in the hyacinth bushes on the side of the house. I ducked and peered around the corner. Rusty stared back at me; his eyes wide and round as an owl's.

11

"Get out of there." I grabbed the neckline of Rusty's striped tee shirt and dragged him from the bushes. "What are you doing skulking around?"

"Nothing." He hung his head. "Rusty heard a noise."

Yeah, I bet he did. Me and Matt falling across the porch like a couple of teenagers. "You've got to stop spying on people, Rusty. It's going to get you into trouble."

He squared his shoulders. "No. Rusty is invisible. Like super hero."

"Really? Because Victoria saw you watching her dress. You scared her and made her boyfriend mad."

"Boyfriend is a bad man. Rusty sees things. Rusty knows things." With a frantic look over his shoulder, he dashed across the street and into the shadows.

"Wait!" He could be a valuable asset in my sleuthing. Plus, his statement stood the hairs on my arms straight up like soldiers. What did he know? What had he seen? Had he witnessed Mrs. Lincoln's murder? I needed to speak with Matt right away.

I sped back to the porch and yanked open the squeaky screen door, smashing into the locked wooden one. "Hey!" Cherokee and Dakota grinned from the other side of the rectangular etched glass. "Not funny."

They proceeded to make kissy faces at each other and pretend to faint. Good grief. Had the whole neighborhood seen our wanton display? "Open this door right now. This is important." They dissolved into hoots of laughter. Fine. There were other ways of getting into the house. I stomped to the kitchen door.

A doggy door, stained with dirt and dog slobber, hung installed by the previous owner. Too small for Sadie, she waited until someone came home to let her out. Now, I'd use it as a means to gain entrance to my own home. It'd be a tight fit, but if I sucked it in and turned sideways, hopefully I could squeeze through. Darn those kids. Where was my mother? Or *their* mother?

I dropped to my hands and knees and stuck my head through the flap. The kids must have decided to watch TV because the volume could be heard all the way to Mars.

Sadie immediately romped across the room and began to wash my face with her oversize tongue. "Stop it. Go away." She increased her slobbering and added a jubilant tail wag. "Somebody come get the dog."

I wiggled my shoulders through the small opening and crawled until my upper torso was through. Yes! I shuffled forward, and stopped. My hips refused to shimmy past the door. Sucking in my gut, I lunged, fighting to grasp a handhold on the wooden floor. Nothing. I tried backing up. Same result. Wonderful. Stuck in the door like a sawed-in-half woman in a magic show. "Help! Stop it, Sadie."

Saliva dripped down my face. I gagged. Why did they have to have the television so loud? I kicked my feet and pounded my fists on the floor. When I'd exhausted myself, I lay still and glared at Sadie. "Why can't you be like Lassie and go for help?"

When I gave up all hope of ever being rescued, somebody tapped me on the back. "Hello?" Matt. Oh, no.

"Not that I don't appreciate the view, but I'm going to open the door. Crawl with it." He chuckled behind me. "Did you know your mother hides a spare key in the birdhouse?"

The door swung open, and I scuttled forward. Tears of relief sprang to my eyes. I would've preferred to be rescued by anyone but Matt, considering my talent for embarrassing myself in front of him, but at this point, a girl couldn't be too picky.

Once Matt stepped inside the house, he squatted down beside me and laughed. "How in the world did you get in this predicament?"

"The kids thought it would be funny to lock me out and I needed to get to a phone. Why are you here?"

"Your Mom called and said somebody was trying to break into the house."

"That was me. Why didn't she come check?"

Mom stepped into the room, the cordless phone to her ear.

"Why didn't you come check?" I asked.

"It's only my daughter. Thank you for your quick response." She pressed the off button and grinned. "After all the hoopla around here, a girl can't be too careful."

"Just get me out of here." I plopped to my stomach. The ridge of the door dug into my ribcage and started to affect my breathing. I hated everybody.

"I'll need a screwdriver and a saw," Matt said, the twinkle in his eye not fading. "You might be a little thing, but you aren't a poodle."

"Ha ha."

Mom nodded and squeezed past us.

A saw? He was going to cut my door. My throat swelled. The beautiful raised-paneled wood. "Isn't there another way? Grease me up or something? Please don't cut my door."

"Afraid not." Matt sat cross-legged next to me. "There won't be much left of the doggy door when I'm done, but that's all I need to destroy."

"I called the fire department," Mom said.

I laid my head on my folded arms.

"Tell me again how you ended up here?" Matt scooted closer. "Why wouldn't somebody open the door? Why was it locked?"

I sniffed and raised my head. "Apparently, everyone—the kids, Rusty, the neighbors, God— saw us rolling around on the porch. Cherokee and Dakota thought it was funny and locked me out.

After you left, I spotted Rusty watching from the bushes and confronted him."

"Watching from the bushes?" Matt frowned.

I nodded. "I told him he shouldn't do that, but the silly man thinks he's invisible. Telling me he sees everything and hears everything. He's going to get into trouble one of these days. You should talk to him. Especially, since I think he might've seen who killed Mrs. Lincoln. That's why I wanted to get to a phone. To call you and tell you what I discovered."

The lines in Matt's forehead deepened. "Were you questioning him?"

Uh-oh. "Not really. He volunteered the info … mainly."

"Stormi, I told you to stay out of this investigation."

"What do you expect me to do when I spot a Peeping Tom? Do the shimmy for his entertainment?" I tried squirming around to find a more comfortable position. What if I had a permanent crease across my middle? I glared at Cherokee and Dakota when they peeked through the kitchen door. Wait until I got my hands around their scrawny necks.

Mom returned and sat at the table, chin propped in hand, and stared at me. "You take after your father. No way could someone like you resemble me. You get into way too much trouble."

Seriously? Mom was the queen of misadventure, and if I were more like Dad, I would have become a police officer rather than an author. "You're kidding, right?"

She shrugged. "I call 'em as I see 'em."

"Mrs. Nelson, could you give us a moment of privacy?" Matt sighed. "Maybe watch for the fire department?"

"Might as well. Angela will be home any minute, and she'll freak out. Most likely think something happened to one of the kids." She shook her head. "If I knew moving in with my daughter would be this dramatic, I might've had second thoughts." With those encouraging words, she shuffled out of sight.

At least I knew how to get rid of my family if I wanted. Keep things hopping around the Nelson homestead. In the distance, sirens wailed. I buried my face again and waited for further embarrassment.

Why couldn't I have left well enough alone? Sitting behind my computer, cranking out mass market paperbacks of sweet romance? But no, I had to listen to my agent and find fodder for my characters. Meat to make my stories fresh. I added a call to her to my mental to-do-list for first thing in the morning.

*

First thing in the morning didn't actually happen until ten. Not after the trauma of being sawed free of my door, gawked at by strangers, apologized over by my niece and nephew, laughed at by my sister when she returned home, and melting into a puddle after another goodbye kiss from Matt. After Sadie gave me a wake-up slurp, I lumbered to the kitchen and poured myself a mug of coffee, heavy on the hot chocolate.

I peeled aside the plastic sheeting that served as my back door and let Sadie out to do her business. I'd have to put a long thin window there to replace the former doggie door. Then, I listened to the quiet house.

Where was everyone? Angela, I knew, started her new job today. The kids, although enrolled, wouldn't be starting school for three more months. A long summer loomed in front of us. And Mom, only God knew what she was up to. I shrugged. Don't look a gift horse in the mouth, so they say. Maybe I could do some writing after I called my agent. I grabbed the cordless phone from the counter and dialed her number.

"Swanson Literary, how may I help you?"

"Elizabeth, it's Stormi." I blew in my chocolate-flavored java.

"What's up? How's the writing going? Do you have a new series for me to pitch?"

"About that." I let her have it with both barrels, then sighed with relief once I'd released all the details except for my kisses with Matt. Some things are private.

Elizabeth's laugh tinkled across the airwaves. "When I told you to up your writing, I didn't mean for you to get involved in a murder investigation."

"I didn't do it on purpose. I thought I'd do some snooping and start writing romantic mysteries with whatever I found out."

"Well, I like the idea, but you can't write anything if you're dead. And, with your family living there, how do you expect to get any writing done? You're going to have to prioritize your time.

Be selfish with it. What's your word count so far?"

"I'm still in the note taking stage."

"Do you have a synopsis?"

"Not yet." My shoulders slumped. "I kind of wanted to wait and see how everything turned out first."

"You're a fiction writer, Stormi. Make it up." She laughed again. "So far, the truth is pretty unbelievable. You've lived in that house for three months and haven't written a word."

"I've written some, besides it takes time to get settled. You have to admit I've got a killer new office."

"Good, now use it. And find a good-looking man to research love scenes with. Yours are all looking the same."

"Right." Mercy. I took a gulp of caffeine. I couldn't help not having a lot of experience in the romance department.

The hot liquid seared the roof of my mouth and tongue. "I gotta go." I hung up and grabbed another glass which I shoved under the spout in the refrigerator door then guzzled the ice water. Aww.

"Rusty!" A woman's voice seeped in the house with the sunshine. "Get out of those bushes."

I rushed to the front window in time to see Matt's sister, Mary Ann, making shooing motions at the neighborhood sneak. I opened the door and stepped on the porch.

Mary Ann turned with a grin and wiggled her eyebrows. "Nice pj's."

I glanced down at the boy shorts and tank top, then ducked back into the house. No sense adding to

Rusty's obsession with underdressed females. "Come on in. Let me change. There's hot coffee on the counter."

I heard the door close as I bounded up the stairs. Within minutes, I tugged on a pair of frayed denim shorts. They might be Daisy Duke's but they were more acceptable than what I was wearing. When I moseyed back into the kitchen, Mary Ann cradled a mug of coffee.

She looked up, a definite twinkle in her eye. "We haven't had a chance to get together yet, and Matt told me what happened last night. I thought I'd come by and make sure you're all right."

Wonderful. The whole neighborhood probably knew by now. I sat in a chair across from her. "Besides bruising my stomach and my ego, I'm fine."

She leaned her elbows on the table and focused on me. "Matt also said you were sticking your nose in places it doesn't belong. Sounds like fun, and I'm always up for a way of getting my brother's dander up. Can I help?"

"Contrary to what Matt thinks, I don't know anything. I'm a prime case of being in the wrong place at the wrong time."

"Maybe not. In the books, the sleuth always makes a list. Do you have one?"

I shook my head. "Not really. Just some things I've jotted down for my book."

"Let's make one right now. Where's the paper?"

"By the fridge."

Mary Ann grabbed a notepad and a pencil. "This'll be fun. Okay. You found Mrs. Lincoln's body. That's important."

"I kind of tripped over her, according to your brother. I remember circling around the body, but I guess that isn't important. I didn't even know there *was* a body."

"Someone bashed you in the head, another good point." The pencil scribbled across the paper like a scorpion. "Any suspects? Have you gone back to the house?"

"No, and yes."

"You must have at least one suspect." Mary Ann frowned, looking so much like her brother, I smiled.

"Well, there's Rusty. The way he sneaks around lends suspicion. And there's Victoria's boyfriend, Bob. He seems capable of violence. Oh, and Mrs. Henley didn't like her very much."

"Good. See, you know more than you think you do. Now, what happened when you went back to the house?"

"It's piled to the rafters with junk, except for Mrs. Lincoln's desk. It looked like she was researching someone's genealogy. But not her own, I don't think. She had Mr. and Mrs. Edgars' name and some others. Maybe some of the neighbors are related?"

She shrugged. "Two more suspects. This is so much fun. Now, we need to find a way to get the neighbors to talk."

I straightened. "I've thought of that. I love to cook, and I have all these casseroles in the freezer. I just need a reason to knock on people's doors. The Neighborhood Watch thing isn't working. Nobody wants to join."

"Well, there you go. Offer them a dish and guilt them into joining. Then, you hold a meeting and talk about what's going on in the neighborhood."

"It could work. Of course, Matt will be there and won't be happy if he suspects us of being nosey. He emphatically told me to stay out of it."

Mary Ann wiggled her eyebrows again. "You let me handle my brother. What's he going to do, arrest his sister?"

12

Mom waltzed into the kitchen, her arms laden with grocery bags. I jumped up to help. "Why didn't you tell me you were going shopping? I would've gone to help."

"No need, dear. I'm not that old." She set her purchases on the counter and smiled at Mary Ann. "Hello, I'm Ann."

"Mary Ann Steele. Looks like we share a name."

"Oh, you're the detective's sister." Mom's gaze flicked to the pad on the table then back to me. "What are y'all doing? Are you working on the case? I thought I was your sidekick."

"I'm sorry." Mary Ann's face flushed. "Obviously, I've stepped on some toes here."

I shook my head. "Relax, Mom. Mary Ann's just giving me a fresh perspective. We're going to deliver meals to the neighbors in order to get them to open up to me."

Mom's eyes widened. "My idea. We talked about it the other night."

Mary Ann's lips thinned. "Maybe I should go."

"This isn't Junior High school." I motioned for

her to remain seated. "I need all the help I can get and not have to worry about soothing battered egos at the same time. Mom, sit down and take a look at the list."

"We already have a list." She plopped into a chair.

"I can't find it."

"That's because I hid it. Wouldn't want the cops to find it, now would we? They'd confiscate it as evidence, and we'd be back to square one."

I rolled my eyes and shrugged at Mary Ann. "Hiding my notes doesn't help." Good grief. Dealing with Mom was like babysitting a five-year-old.

A light breeze rattled the plastic on the door, carrying with it the light scent of honeysuckle. Sadie barked once, and tore past the window in pursuit of a red-tailed squirrel. Good, she was getting her exercise without me having to walk her.

"So, are we willing to work together?" I gave Mom a stern look.

"Fine."

Mary Ann clapped her hands. "We'll be like the three Musketeers."

"More like the three Stooges," I said.

I opened the freezer and took stock. There hadn't been a lot of opportunity for my favorite pastime lately. "Okay, to name a few, I have a French onion chicken casserole, an oven-baked spaghetti dish, and some stuffed peppers. I'd planned on using them for meals this week, but I can cook more. Where do we want to go first?"

Mom's eyes lit up. "We can call ourselves the

Welcome Wagon."

"Name's taken." I closed the freezer.

"Well, we have to have a name." She crossed her arms and sulked.

"How about the Hickory Hellos?" Mary Ann giggled. "Considering you live on Hickory."

"Works for me." I resumed my seat. Great, another self-appointed committee to devote time to and keep me from working. "But, remember, our main objective is to get people to join the Neighborhood Watch. Then, gain their trust and pick their brains." At this rate, I'd never get my book written. I definitely needed to set up a schedule.

Mom raised her hand. Maybe I *was* dealing with school children.

"Yes?"

"I did find out Mrs. Lincoln wasn't very well liked." She looked like the proverbial cat that swallowed the canary.

"Well?"

"Let me fix us some tea first."

Mary Ann and I sighed in unison. Obviously, Mom would milk the details for as long as possible.

By the time she set three iced teas on the table, my impatience level reached the ceiling. "Is there anything else before you tell us your news?"

"Oh. Little Debbies." She grabbed a box of lemon cakes from one of the bags and dumped it on a plate. "There. I wish I would have had time to bake something, but I didn't know we were having company."

"Mother, please. I'm growing old waiting on

you."

She folded her hands on the table. High spots of color resided on both cheeks. She leaned forward and lowered her voice. "Seems Mrs. Lincoln was a bit of a Nosey Nelly."

"Like someone else I know?"

She frowned. "I know you aren't talking about me. I always mind my own business. Anyway, she butted into people's personal lives, even going so far as to look into their bloodlines. Being a direct descendent of Oak Meadows' founding fathers, she felt she had the right. Even tried to get poor Rusty arrested or run out of town because he was undesirable. Her words, not mine."

"Where did you get this information?" I shifted my glance from Mary Ann, who listened with eyes as big as saucers, back to my mother.

"A couple of people, actually. Amazing how people come up and talk when you're puttering in the yard."

I glanced out the window. No yard work done that I could see. "What were you doing?"

"Pretending to pull weeds in the flower beds out front. It was very relaxing. I might do it for real next time. Anyway ..." She shoved a slice of cake in her mouth, chewed for eternity, and then swallowed. "Marion Henley was the most talkative, but the Olsons stopped by, too. You know I have one of those faces that invites confidence."

Huh. I gnawed my inner lip. Mom had a high opinion of herself, but she was right. People did talk to her. They'd probably talk to Mary Ann, too, with her being Matt's sister, or maybe not for the same reason. They might think she would tell her brother everything they said. Me, being the trashy romance novel author people believed I was, took some getting used to. They probably worried I'd write about them.

"In my way of thinking," Mom continued like one of those dolls whose pull string was stuck, "I ought to be the spy of this little operation. Y'all can do the heavy thinking, and I'll do the talking."

"I vote Stormi as the bodyguard." Mary Ann lifted her glass in a toast. "Matt told me how you hit Bob with a flashlight. Brilliant. You're lucky he didn't press charges, though."

Mom raised her tea. "Out of character, too. My daughter's afraid of her own shadow."

True, but I thought the man was going to hit me. Something I dislike more than things that go bump in the night. I ducked my head, not wanting to share glory where it wasn't due. I'd acted without thinking about the consequences. If Matt hadn't shown up, things could've gone from bad to horrible.

Yep, I definitely missed my tame romance novels. Shut away in my office, I'd let the world continue along on its own, occasionally venturing out for book signings or conferences. But then, I mingled with people of my own kind. Not murderers and women who didn't trust their men past the front door. A horn honked, drawing my attention to the window.

Rusty meandered down the sidewalk, his head whipping back and forth so fast it's a wonder it didn't fall off. The guy appeared to glance in every window he passed. The man needed to be watched for sure.

"Where does Rusty live?" I asked.

"Over the garage at Mrs. Henley's," Mary Ann said. "I think he's the son of a deceased friend of hers."

"What does he do for a living?"

"Odd jobs here and there."

I bolted from my seat and out the front door. "Rusty."

He jerked and whirled to face me, with his hands rubbing at his military crew. "Yeah?"

"Sorry to startle you." I stopped to catch my breath. "How are you at yard work?"

"Rusty is good."

"Wonderful. What will you charge to get my lawn up to standard and keep it that way?"

"Ten dollars a month."

I grinned. How many people took advantage of Rusty's lack of skill with numbers or his comprehension of the value of money? Well, it wouldn't be me. "How about eighty dollars a month?"

He sighed. "That's not very much, but Rusty will do it."

"Great. Tools are in the shed in the back." I crossed my arms and narrowed my eyes. "But you stay out of my house. Understand? Don't go near my sister or my niece." I still thought the man relatively harmless, but there was nothing wrong with being cautious.

I hoped the state of my yard would keep him busy for a while before someone took offense to him staring through their windows and did actually get him tossed in jail. "And no more peeking in people's windows."

"But Rusty sees things."

"Yeah, but it's wrong." I gave him another stern look and waved him toward the backyard. He shuffled off with his head down. Hopefully, I was doing a good deed and not setting myself up for frustration. The last thing I needed was another person to look after.

A grinding noise filled the air. I stuck my head over the fence to peer into the Edgar's yard. Herman shoved sticks into a wood chipper as fast as the machine could work. I glanced around my yard, relieved to discover nothing that needed to be shoved into something with large whirling teeth. For sure, I'd be an accident waiting to happen.

He caught me spying and nodded. With a sheepish grin, I waved and withdrew. The Edgars got my vote for the unfriendliest neighbors. Maybe I should take them a casserole, too? They looked Italian. Maybe spaghetti? Or would that be too cliché?

I turned toward the house and stopped. Shivers skipped up my spine.

Matt marched toward me, a sullen Dakota at his side.

13

All I needed was to have my nephew marched home by Matt. What else could go wrong? "What happened?"

"I've had complaints from the neighbors about your nephew skateboarding on the sidewalks and badgering people about Mrs. Lincoln," Matt said. "This has got to stop, Stormi. Your family cannot keep sticking their noses into my investigation."

"I didn't tell him, too." I gave Dakota my sternest look. "What do you have to say for yourself?"

"I just want to help. This place is so boring." Dakota huffed. "What's it hurting anyway? The old bat is dead. I can't hurt her none by asking questions."

"Have some respect." Matt shook his head. "Do I have your word, Stormi, that you will deal with this matter?"

"We'll take care of it." Mom grabbed her grandson by the arm and marched him toward the house. "So, did you learn anything?"

My eyes widened. I knew what her question really meant and hoped Matt hadn't caught on.

From the scowl on his face, he had. He sighed. "Tell my sister I'll wait for her at home."

"How did you know she was here?"

"She told me. I suppose you're roping her into your mystery business, too."

"Nobody is roping me into anything." Mary Ann stepped off the porch. "I want to help. I haven't had this much fun in a long time." She grinned, dimples winking from her cheeks. "Don't be mad, and if you insist on pouting, do it at home by yourself."

He started to turn and walk away, then stopped and marched up the steps to the front door. "I might as well hear what the boy has to say."

I grinned. Mister Stern Detective was every bit as curious as the rest of us. If he would only realize that we could help him solve the murder of Mrs. Lincoln, his job would be a lot easier. The police department should really loosen up a bit and let the public help them. I followed my crowd into the house and took a seat around the kitchen table.

Matt grabbed the notes off the table before anyone could stop him. "A pretty elaborate list. I'm impressed. Dakota, *did* you learn anything?"

My nephew grabbed a chocolate-chip cookie from a plate on the counter and stuffed it into his mouth, raining crumbs down the front of his tank top. "Nobody liked her, and I mean nobody."

"That's nothing new." Matt crossed his arms.

"She was always calling the HOA on people, yet her yard is the worst in the neighborhood." Dakota grabbed another cookie and waved it to emphasize his point. "I'm thinking someone got tired of her complaining and silenced her. Not to mention the fact that she was nosing into other people's history."

Matt stiffened. "What do you mean?"

"I think he means exactly what Mom and I discovered during one of our trips to the house. Mrs. Lincoln had a website on genealogy on her desktop computer. Not unnatural except for the fact that it wasn't her name she was researching." I cocked my head and grinned. "It was Mrs. Henley's. Not only that, there was a list of other neighbors on a piece of paper near the computer."

He twisted his mouth while thinking. After several long seconds of staring at me, he finally broke the silence. "How did the department miss that?"

I shrugged. "Incompetence?"

"Lemonade." Mom plopped a tray of drinks on the table. "Everyone thinks better while hydrated."

"The police department is not incompetent. I'm in charge of the investigation and I take offense to that." Matt grabbed a glass. "You can rest assured I'll be looking into why no one noticed what you did."

"So, you're admitting that Mom and I found something valuable."

"Yes, but you broke the law doing it. Stay out of Mrs. Lincoln's house." Matt sipped the lemonade and puckered. Mom always did make her lemonade a bit on the tart side, but considering his sister's was worse, he should be able to muddle through.

"We don't have any other reason to go there." Mom patted him on the shoulder. "Too sour?"

"No, perfect." Matt took a bigger sip. "I'm just used to Mary Ann's which is like drinking straight lemon juice."

"It is not." Mary Ann tossed a napkin at him.

"I know some other things," Dakota said. "Like, people are getting mad at that guy who keeps peeking in windows. I guess he knows a lot of secrets." With those words, Dakota stuck his ear buds in his ear and dashed out the back door.

Poor Rusty. There seemed to be a lot going on in his head. The problem was getting him to verbalize it. If someone could draw the information out of him, they could probably find out the identity of the killer with no other snooping involved. I needed to figure out a way to get inside his head.

"What do you ladies have planned next?" Matt reached for one of the cookies. I could tell his question took everything in him to ask. He hated the idea that we might actually be able to dig up valuable information.

"We're starting up the Hickory Hellos." Mom flung open the freezer. "My daughter has a stack of frozen casseroles just waiting to be eaten. We're going to make the rounds around the neighborhood, drop off a casserole, and ask people about their concerns. You never know. We might find something."

"You never know." Matt stood. "I've given up telling you to stay out of things, so all I'm going to ask now is that you be careful and don't step over the line of the law." He gave me a small smile and headed out the back door in the same direction Dakota had gone.

"That's the best go ahead signal you'll get from my brother," Mary Ann said.

"He seems ... mad." I slumped in my chair. The last thing I wanted was for Matt to be mad at me. I sure would miss his kisses if he wanted nothing more to do with me.

"He'll get over it. I'm always going against his orders." Mary Ann giggled. 'The poor thing has always been outnumbered by women. You'd think he'd be used to losing the battles by now."

I drummed my fingers on the table and stared out the kitchen window. Matt leaned against the fence, talking to ... well, since I couldn't see anyone, I assumed he was talking to Rusty. Which proved my point. Getting information out of the poor man was going to be next to impossible.

"Earth to Stormi." Mary Ann waved a napkin in front of my face. "You're far away. Dreaming of my brother?"

"What? No." Even if I was, I couldn't let his younger sister know. I'd never hear the end of it. "I'm just wondering how we can get the information that's locked inside Rusty's head."

We all sat at the table, chins in our hands, and tried to come up with a solution. "I got nothing," I said.

"We need to look at the situation as if we were interviewing a child." Mom stood and headed for the window. "Matt's gone, which probably means Rusty is, too." She turned back to us. "If Rusty saw something he shouldn't, don't you think he'd be dead by now? What if he doesn't really understand what it is he saw? Could be anything or nothing. I don't think we should put all our eggs in his basket. Bless his heart, but he's a few yolks short."

"Don't be mean." I scooted my chair back and stood. "I'm going to take Sadie for a walk to clear my head. I'll cook supper when I get back. Mary Ann, you're welcome to stay."

"No, I'll walk with you as far as my house. Matt and I take turns cooking and it's my turn." Mary Ann tapped her forefinger on the notes. "Don't fret. We'll think of something, and don't forget we'll be delivering casseroles."

Which meant I needed to do some more cooking. Mom was good, but I was better. She excelled at baking, though. Maybe desserts would be better. Everyone liked chocolate, right? "The Hickory Hellos will hand out cakes and pies, instead."

"That's a great idea." Mom clapped. "I'll get started baking right away."

I clipped the leash to Sadie's collar and headed out the front door, Mary Ann beside me. "Don't look now," she said, "but Rusty is watching from the bushes, again."

"I've told him that is unacceptable behavior. Rusty!" I stomped my foot. "Come here."

"Rusty is getting the lawn mower." He slunk from the bushes.

"Don't lie. We've discussed this before. If you want to talk to me, then ring the doorbell."

"Yes. But Rusty sees—"

"I know. You see things." I wrapped Sadie's leash around my wrist. "Are you ready to tell me what you saw?"

He shook his head. "Things. Bad things."

I sighed. "Give me a name."

"Rusty."

"A bad name, not yours."

He scratched his head. He seemed to think so hard he looked like he was in pain. "I don't know." He glanced toward the Edgars' house, then across the street to where Mrs. Olson watched us, her arms crossed, and a leaf blower in her hand. "That woman is angry." He dashed around the corner of the house.

"Impossible." The task before me, all to garner the fodder for a book, was overwhelming. "The one possible witness we have can't form a coherent sentence."

"Don't give up on him." Mary Ann glared at Mrs. Olson. "He's a good guy, even if he is strange. Eventually he'll say something. Oh, that woman is ridiculous." She gave a wave of her fingers. "Matt tells me to stop antagonizing her, but seriously … I've never given her reason to think I want her husband."

"It must be sad to be that insecure." We stopped in front of Mary Ann's house. Her hunky shirtless brother pushed a lawnmower across the front lawn. It should be a crime to look that good when you were sweaty and covered with grass clippings.

Matt caught me staring and waved. Mary Ann laughed and skipped up the steps toward her front door with a promise to stop by in a few days to compare notes. I returned Matt's wave and tugged on Sadie's leash. The dog seemed as enamored as I was by Matt. The only difference between us, other than she had more hair, was the fact that my tongue wasn't hanging quite so far out as hers.

By the time we circled the cul-de-sac, Mrs. Olson had returned to her house. The screeching of a harpy ripped through the open window. Sadie's ears perked as she cowered against my leg.

"You big scaredy cat." I patted her head. "And you so big, too."

When a man's voice joined in the screaming, I stopped to listen. After all, as the president of the Neighborhood Watch, I had a certain obligation to make sure things didn't escalate out of control. Even Matt across the street had stopped his lawn work to listen, so I was only doing my civic duty, right?

Mrs. Olson was on a rampage about her husband making eyes at every woman under the age of fifty. Topping the list was me, Mary Ann, and Victoria Lanham. I stifled the urge to pound on her door and tell her the only men I was interested in were the heroes in my books and the hunky detective across the street. Instead, I tugged on Sadie's leash the second the woman stepped back on her porch while brandishing a broom.

Sadie and I continued our stroll, waving at neighbors I had met and those I hadn't. Since our gated community consisted of three streets, I made a mental note to find time to meet the residents of the other two streets. But first, I needed to start my new book.

With all the goings on so far, I had plenty for the first few chapters. All I lacked was the murderer. If I didn't find out who it was soon, I would make one up. It could be any of my neighbors, after all, and since I was changing the names anyway, I wouldn't be damaging anyone's reputation. It wasn't like any of them would actually read the book. Not if it came from a romance writer, anyway.

In front of my house, I spotted Angela turning into the driveway. She sat in her idling Prius for a few minutes while she talked into her cell phone. When did she get a Prius? I thought she was broke.

I hurried and knocked on her window. She shrieked and dropped her phone. After fumbling on the floor to locate it, she turned off the ignition and shoved the door open. "You scared me. Why are you skulking around with that beast anyway?"

"Where did you get the new car?" I took note of the black pencil skirt and burgundy blouse. "Are those new clothes?"

"I traded in the minivan and yes, this is a new outfit. I have a job now and need to look professional."

"I thought you were broke."

"I am." She narrowed her eyes and shifted a new Coach purse higher on her shoulder. "Are you trying to get rid of us? You have this big house all to yourself. It isn't like we're hurting you or anything."

True, but it *was* my house and I had yet to do any writing since they'd moved in. Not totally their fault since I found it necessary to solve a crime, but the idea that my older sister might be mooching off me didn't sit right. Still, she was right. I had a house that had plenty of room. I needed to prioritize and ask the others to respect my privacy.

"I'm going inside to grab something to eat. You can continue walking that giant of a dog and peeking in people's windows." She stomped up the stairs and into the house.

"I don't peek in windows. That would be Rusty!" I shouted after her. I snuck into houses in the name of research. Big difference.

I looped Sadie's leash around the porch post and then sat in the swing. It was too nice of an evening to sit inside. If Mom didn't mind, I'd have my supper out here.

Torie strolled by, arm-in-arm with her boyfriend, Bob. She peered into his face like a woman in love. He looked down on her like a man who cherished his woman. Maybe their fight the other night had been a fluke, a rare occurrence. At the end of the street, Bob gave her a long kiss, a pat on the rear, and headed through the gates of the community into the wide world outside Oak Meadow Estates.

Marion Henley stood in her canary-yellow house dress and watched the proceedings with a scowl on her face. The Olsons had finally stopped shouting next door, and on the other side of the house, the Edgars left their porch and headed around the corner of their house without a wave or a nod to anyone. Seemed as if the whole street was out enjoying the nice evening.

A couple I had yet to meet, strolled hand-in-hand down the sidewalk. The woman who appeared to be around fifty and had hair the same shade as Lucille Ball, patted the shoulder of a man slightly older, and stopped in front of my house. "Are you the author?"

"Yes." I stopped the swing and stood. "I'm Stormi Nelson."

"I have a manuscript I'd like you to look at." She hefted a tapestry tote bag off her companion's shoulder. "We're Sarah and Ben Thompson. This is a steamy novel. It should be right up your alley." She approached me and set the bag at my feet. "One hundred and ten thousand words of sheer brilliance. Contains romance, murder, intrigue, all written from personal experience, so it should ring true to the readers. I left my card in there, too, so you can call me with your thoughts."

"But, I—"

"Thanks. Can't talk now. Got some dirty business to take care of." She wiggled her fingers and headed down the street with her man.

I sighed. One of the pitfalls of being a writer was wannabes wanting you to read their stuff. I plopped back onto the swing and pushed the bag aside with my foot. I'd have to come up with a nice way of turning her down.

I was still sitting there thirty minutes later when Mom brought me a plate of chicken strips and French fries. "Homemade," she said. "None of that fast food stuff."

"Thank you. I could have come inside and got my food."

"I was coming out anyway." She settled in a wicker rocker across from me and balanced a plate on her knees. "It's a beautiful evening. I spotted several of the neighbors taking advantage of the cooler than normal temperatures."

I told her about the wannabe writer. "She didn't let me get a word in edgewise. Now, I need to come up with a tactful way of telling her I don't read other people's manuscripts."

"Good luck with that. I've always thought about writing a book."

I groaned.

"Don't worry. I won't ask you to read it and tell me whether it's any good. I suspect readers will do a good enough job of that."

Rusty sprinted down the middle of the street, arms pumping, eyes wide. I pushed to my feet and headed toward him. "Rusty."

He stopped and whirled to face me. "Rusty didn't do it."

"Do what?" My heart stopped. The front of his tee shirt was covered with blood.

"Kill Torie."

14

"Mom, please go get Matt." I took Rusty by the arm and led him to my porch steps. "Sit here while we find someone to help you." I glanced down the road in the direction Torie had gone earlier. Please, God, don't let Rusty be the killer. He'd never survive prison.

Five minutes later, Matt dashed to our side, quickly pulling on a dark tee shirt, and was followed a few seconds later by my panting mother. She sagged against the porch rail and let Matt kneel beside Rusty.

"What happened?" Matt tilted Rusty's head so the young man would have to look at him. "Where is Victoria?"

"The alley."

Matt yanked a cell phone from his pocket and called for backup. "Stay with him." He dashed away.

"I'm going. Mom, stay with him."

Her mouth fell open. "What if he's the killer?"

"Rusty did not kill her." He opened his mouth and wailed.

I shook my head and raced in the direction Matt

went, leaving behind a crying Rusty, a whining mother, and a barking dog. I couldn't get away fast enough.

Whirling around the corner behind the houses across the street from mine, I skidded to a stop beside a battered green Dumpster. Matt stared at the body of Torie Lanham. Her once beautiful features were pulled into a look of terror. Instead of gardening shears, a kitchen butcher knife protruded from her chest. I wasn't experienced enough to determine whether it could be the same person who killed Mrs. Lincoln, but I'd bet my laptop it was.

"I told you to stay put." Matt sounded weary. "Who is watching Rusty?"

"My mom." I sidled up next to him as tears stung my eyes. "What a waste. Who do you think killed her?"

"Too early to tell."

"I guess you could go house-to-house and see who has a set of knives that match that one." I leaned down for a closer look. "I've seen that style at Wal-Mart. They're good knives, surprisingly. Can cut right through a chicken with little problem. I know this, because we have the same set. Most likely, a lot of people do."

"This is not the time to compare kitchen cutlery, Stormi." Matt frowned and shook his head. "A young woman is dead."

Since they weren't appreciated, I decided to keep my mental notes to myself for a while. While Matt made notations in a small notebook, I studied the area surrounding the victim. Several sets of footprints scuffed the gravel alley. I had no way of knowing whether they were made yesterday, last week, or moments before. Blood sprayed the side of the Dumpster... no question where that came from.

"Rusty is covered with blood."

Matt whirled at my words. "Say that again."

"I'm surprised you didn't notice. Rusty's shirt is covered with blood. He came running up the street, saying he didn't kill her."

"Hard to see what's on his shirt when he's sitting in the shadow of your porch. Call your mother and have her try to bring Rusty here. Tell her that Matt wants to talk to him. Hopefully, he'll come."

I pulled my phone from my pocket, glad for once I'd remembered to bring it, and dialed Mom. By the time she and Rusty arrived on the heels of the ambulance and police, most of the neighborhood had also congregated at the mouth of the alley.

"This is turning into a circus." Matt yelled for one of the other officers to keep the crowd back.

I moved aside before he ordered me behind the yellow crime scene tape another officer was stringing. Mom kept trying to catch my attention by waving one hand, while she kept a tight grip on the sleeve of Rusty's shirt with the other. No way was I leaving my spot. Matt wanted Rusty, he could go get him. If I moved, I might miss something important.

Matt motioned for one of the officers to bring Rusty across the line. Rusty cowered and tried to pull back, until Matt went to fetch him himself. He planted the young man next to me and ordered him to stay. "I mean it. I'll be right back."

Tears streamed down Rusty's face, leaving tracks in an incredibly dirty face. He groaned and wrapped his arms around his middle, tucking his chin into his chest.

"Do you know who killed Torie?" I bent to peer into his eyes.

He nodded.

"Can you tell me?"

"Bad people."

Here we go again. "Yes, they are very bad. Are they neighbors?"

He nodded.

"More than one?"

He nodded again. I wanted to clap. Finally, we were getting somewhere. I now knew there was most likely a guilty couple rather than a single person, which ruled out the most likely culprit— Torie's boyfriend, Bob. "Do you know their names? Was it Mrs. Olson?"

"Stop badgering the witness." Matt stepped between us. "Rusty, I need you to go to the station with me and a nice woman is going to ask you some questions. Okay?"

"Can I have ice cream?" Rusty lifted his head.

"You sure can." Matt guided him toward a squad door, me hot on their heels.

"He said it was a couple of bad people. That narrows it down, don't you think? He also said it was one of the neighbors. I could be the woman who questions him."

"Leave it alone, Stormi. I'll take into consideration what you've told me," he said facing me. "But you are a civilian. Not a police officer. Let us handle this before you get yourself into trouble."

"Do you mean trouble as in with the law or trouble as in danger?"

"Both." He put his hands on my shoulders. "Please. I can't solve these murders and worry about my girl, too."

His girl? I grinned and nodded. At that moment, I'd promise him anything, especially when his handsome face was creased with worry because he cared about me.

"Good. Now, go home. I'll stop by tomorrow and tell you what I can. I know you'll go snooping if I don't." He kissed the tip of my nose, making my knees weak, and held the crime scene tape up so I could duck under.

Once Torie's body was loaded into the ambulance and most of the nosey neighbors had left, I waved at Rusty through the window of the squad car and walked home with Mom. I wouldn't be falling asleep for a while, not after seeing Torie that way or the despair on Rusty's face. Instead, I would use the time to put the thoughts in my head onto paper.

Mom was surprisingly silent on the way home. Inside the house, she headed straight for the coffee pot and started making a pot. "Get out your notepad," she said. "I noticed a few things while I was surveying the crowd."

I grabbed the pad from the counter, located a partially sharpened pencil, and sat at the kitchen table. "I didn't see a whole lot at the crime scene. Too many footprints and I couldn't tell whether they were new or old. There was blood splatter on the Dumpster, but that fit the way poor Torie died. Hopefully, you have something more workable."

"I believe I do." She pressed the button on the coffee maker and sat across from me. "Every one of our neighbors was there. Even Mr. and Mrs. Congeniality from next door. The part I found strange though was that the whole time the police were taking care of Torie, Mrs. Olson was grinning. Not a sad smile either. I'm talking about an ear to ear grin. No sadness happening there.

"The Edgars whispered among themselves, which I found strange, and Bob was absent. Then, there's poor Rusty. He kept mumbling about the bad man and woman. That's all I could get out of him, but that tells us it's a couple."

"I saw Bob leave the community when I was walking the dog." Thankfully, Angela had let the dog inside. Sadie now rested her giant head on my feet. "Rusty pretty much told me it wasn't a single person either. But where does this leave us? We still don't know who the killer is, and just because the poor boy says it's more than one person, doesn't mean it necessarily is.."

Mom drummed her fingers on the table, only to jump up when the aromatic smell of coffee filled the kitchen. "What worries me is—" She reached into the cabinet and pulled down two mugs. "that another person has been murdered. What if the killers come after us? We can't keep it a secret that we're snooping." She poured the coffee and carried the mugs to the table, then grabbed flavored cream from the refrigerator.

"True." I glanced at my notes. At some point I'd

circled the fact that Mrs. Lincoln had been digging into ancestry. I also couldn't shake the fact that it might not have been her own genealogy she was looking at. Oh, yeah. There had been two circled names on the paper in her office, Rusty and the Edgars. "Mom, it's very possible the police already have the murderer in custody."

"You're talking about that poor boy again." She shook her head. "I find it hard to imagine, but you might be right. I've heard tell of people like him not really knowing right from wrong, something snaps, and WHAM a dead person. But that boy seemed genuinely frightened."

"Because he realized what he had done?" I stirred mocha flavored creamer into my coffee.

"I don't know. It seems too easy. I think we should go back to our plan of taking desserts to people and fishing for information."

Maybe Mom was right. Somebody on our street was a two-time murderer. The only way we were going to find them was to catch them in the act. By taking desserts and asking questions, we would put a target on our back that even a child couldn't miss. I shuddered, all bravery fleeing.

I glanced across the table at Mom's lovely face. Slightly round with only a wrinkle or two, her auburn hair pulled back into a barrette, she was still lovely at the age of fifty. The shadow of missing Dad sometimes passed across her features, but otherwise her loveliness and willingness to accept any new person as "friend" should have her single days ending soon. After two years, it was surprising she didn't have a male friend.

My hand trembled as I lifted my coffee mug. What if she never got another chance at love? With a murderer running loose, and the two of us snooping among the neighbors, it was very possible she could be the next victim. I couldn't let that happen. Frightened or not, target on my back or not, I had to make sure my family remained safe from the foolish choice I made to solve a crime for the sake of a new book.

Yes, Matt was a detective, and I had full belief he was capable of solving the murders, but cops had to do things by the book. I didn't. I studied Mom through lower lashes. How could I investigate without her tagging along? What about Angela, Dakota, and Cherokee? They were all in danger, too, as long as I pursued this path.

"Forget it." Mom slammed her mug on the table. "Your face is still as easy to read as those books you write."

"What are you talking about?" I focused on my coffee.

"You're worried about your family. Well, stop it." She reached across the table and laid a hand on mine. "I'm in this just as much as you are, and I don't plan on any stupid killer putting a stop to me or mine. Got it?"

"You might not have a choice. I doubt Mrs. Lincoln and Torie were surprised by a random act of violence. Their murders were premeditated. They were hunted down and killed." I leaned down and patted the head of the new friend I gained with the death of an old woman.

"We are on our guard. Until the killer is found, I

don't trust a single soul. I promise to go nowhere alone." She jumped up and stretched to grab a bag from the top of the refrigerator. "I almost forgot." She dumped the bag on the table. Three Tasers tumbled out. "There's one for each of us. Don't leave home without it."

"Yay! I've always wanted one of these." Now, who could I tase to see how they actually worked on a person? For research, of course.

Thunder boomed outside. I jumped, splashing my coffee and dropping my new toy. "I didn't know it was going to rain today." I loved storms. I shoved the Taser into the pocket of my cotton capris and refilled my mug. If there was a storm coming, I wanted to be on the front porch.

The wind immediately buffeted me, almost slamming me onto the swing. Lightening slashed the sky. I counted. One...Two...Three...BOOM. Excitement leaped in my chest. I snuggled under an afghan that had miraculously stayed on the swing despite the wind and watched the rain race across the sky in our direction.

I breathed deep, loving the clean scent of a rainy evening. Leaning my head against the back of the swing, I let the storm wash away my fears, if only for an hour or two.

Up and down the street lights flicked off. I seemed to be the only one still awake at ten p.m. Except for Mom, of course. She joined me on the porch wearing a dark hoodie. At least I didn't have to worry about her traipsing the neighborhood in this kind of weather. She took her usual seat in the rocking chair and set it into motion with a push of her foot.

Down the street strolled a tall figure in a dark raincoat. He, or she, stopped in front of our house. Mom and I froze. I slipped my hand into my pocket as slowly as possible and slid out the Taser. Why didn't I take it out of its packaging before coming outside? Did I learn nothing from my thoughts in the kitchen?

I tore at the hard plastic with my teeth as the stranger came closer. When that didn't work, I balanced the package on my leg and pulled, my arms going up and down like a water pump. "Come on." I stood and ripped harder.

"What are you doing?" Matt bounded up the stairs and removed his hood, shaking his hair like a wet dog.

"You almost gave us a heart attack." Mom shook her head. "Stormi was going to tase you."

"Really?" He laughed. "It's still in its packaging." He flipped open a pocketknife and took the package from me. "What are you doing with this anyway?"

"It's for protection." I resumed my seat. My heart pounded a mile a minute. "Why are you out walking in this kind of weather?"

"I love storms."

"Seems like we all do, considering I named my youngest daughter after one. She was born during a real humdinger. Can I get you a cup of coffee?" Mom reached for the door handle.

"That would be great, thanks." Matt sat next to me and handed me the Taser. "I'm glad you have this, but regret the fact you feel you need one."

"In my quest for a new story, I've put myself and my family at risk." Tears clogged my throat. "I have no idea how to stop the avalanche."

"Stop nosing around." He put his arm around my shoulder and pulled me close. Rain from his coat soaked into my afghan, but I didn't care. His touch warmed me, made me feel safe.

"What happened to Rusty?"

"They're keeping him overnight, but have to let him go in the morning. We have nothing on him and can't get a word out of him. Since we don't know yet whether the blood on his shirt belongs to Torie or someone else, that's a dead end, too, until results come back."

"Do you think he killed her?" I peered into his face.

"No." He sighed. "He's not the smartest guy, but Torie wasn't dumb. I'm pretty sure she could have gotten away from him. He moves like a turtle."

"Unless he had just found a dead body." Rusty had run down the road pretty fast when I stopped him. He must be terrified behind bars. "Does he have a ride home in the morning?"

"His landlady will pick him up. Mrs. Henley is pretty protective of the poor guy. She's probably the only one he will talk to, and she has promised to try and help us find out what he knows."

The proverbial light bulb went off over my head. Of course, she would know. Tomorrow, I'd pay the lovely, gossipy, woman a visit.

"Here you go." Mom joined us and handed Matt his coffee.

He straightened, pulling his arm free and leaving me chilled, and accepted the mug. "I'm surprised to see you two up this late."

"Stormi has always gone outside when it rains. I got into the habit of joining her when I could when she would sneak out when she was younger." Mom settled back on her rocker. "Total opposites, my two daughters. If I were to check, I'm sure I'd find Angela under the covers. Much like that monster you call a dog. She's cowering under the table and whining every time it thunders."

Some watchdog she would be, but I had grown to love the sweet thing. "At least she isn't in a dog house like the first time I met her. Too bad, Sadie can't talk. She could definitely tell us who the killer is."

15

The first thing I wanted to do the next morning was visit Mrs. Henley, but I planted my rear in my office chair and wrote two thousand words in my new book, *Anything For A Story*. Satisfied with the day's productivity, I whipped off an email to my agent letting her know I'd actually started the book, then rummaged in my closet for something cute to wear.

Mom was right. I dressed like a child. If I wanted Matt to look at me with romance in his eyes, I needed to dress like a woman. I had nothing to wear. I settled on a pair of denim walking shorts and a pale blue tank top that matched my eyes. At the first opportunity, I would hit the mall in Little Rock. I could afford the clothes, but I enjoyed being frugal and didn't see the sense in a closet full of clothes when I spent most of my time holed up in my office.

The house was quiet when I went downstairs. Angela was most likely at work, and while I was interested in where my niece and nephew might be, I didn't want to incur their wrath by opening their bedroom doors and waking them if they were still sleeping. So … that left Mom. I glanced out the front window, not surprised to see her chatting it up with Mrs. Henley. Rusty was hard at work weeding my flower bed.

After grabbing a pop tart from the pantry, and a small bottle of orange juice, I moved outside to greet Rusty. "Good morning. How are you?"

"Rusty fine."

"Not traumatized from your night in jail?"

"Huh?" He glanced up with a frown. "Jail was cold."

I shrugged. "Nice work on the flower bed. I like the petunias." I smiled and went across the street to join Mom and Mrs. Henley.

"The poor dear smelled to high heaven and hadn't touched a bit of his breakfast. He hates oatmeal." Mrs. Henley crossed her arms. "Those jailers said he had to eat what they provided or go hungry. Why can't people understand he isn't like the rest of us?"

She seemed awfully concerned for a mere landlord. There was something more to her relationship with Rusty other than landlord and tenant. "Is Rusty your son?" I asked.

She stiffened for a moment, then blinked back tears. "Yes, he is. I gave him up at birth and reconnected with him several years ago when I offered him a room over my garage. He was never adopted. He grew up in shelters and foster homes." She covered her face with her hands. "I've lived with the guilt ever since."

"Does he know?" I glanced over my shoulder to where Rusty shoved weeds into a black lawn bag.

"I've told him, but he doesn't understand. We're

both content to leave things at Mrs. Henley and Rusty, for now. He got a bit of joy out of us having the same last name, but it hasn't gone any further than that." She wiped her eyes on the sleeve of her green housedress. The neon pink flowers scattered across the forest green background made me wish for my sunglasses.

"Have you talked to him about the murders?" I asked. "He knows something important that could help the police."

"I've asked him. He won't say a word. Oh, I wish he'd stop the Peeping Tom stuff. It's going to get him killed."

Mom put an arm around her shoulders. "We'll do our best to make sure that doesn't happen. Could the two of you go on vacation somewhere? At least until this all blows over?"

"We've nowhere to go. I live on a fixed income." She waved her arm. "Don't let the house fool you. I inherited it. We're stuck here for the long haul." She whirled to face me, a hard glint in her eyes. "You get that boyfriend of yours to solve this thing, you hear?"

"He's doing his best." Now, I had one more reason to solve the murders:. To keep Rusty alive and his already guilt-stricken mother to not suffer more grief. Maybe I could come up with enough chores around my house to keep Rusty busy until dark each night. It also didn't sound as if Mrs. Henley was a suspect in the murder of Mrs. Lincoln or Torie, but I wasn't ruling her out completely. I didn't have that many suspects to begin with. Surely, I could narrow it down before too long, unless everybody died and only one suspect was left. That would really stink.

"What time is Rusty home each night?" I asked.

"He's a grown man," Mrs. Henley said. "He doesn't have a curfew."

I gave her a look that said, "Yeah, right."

"Fine. He's supposed to be in his bed by nine every night."

"Then I'll keep him busy working every night until then. That should keep him out of trouble."

Her look softened. "That is sweet of you. Now, if you two ladies don't mind, I have work to do in my vegetable garden. Have a good day." She turned and left.

"Well, that got us nowhere." Mom turned and surveyed the street.

"Not true. We learned that Rusty is her son, and she'll do anything to keep him safe."

"You're saying she could have killed those two people?"

"Maybe, if they threatened her son she could have. We can't rule it out." I scanned the street along with my mother. No one was puttering around in their yards. I had no idea what move to make next. "Still want to do the baking?"

"I have no idea. I'm at a loss. I guess if you manage to keep Rusty busy, and someone else dies, we know he didn't do it. Which is a cold-hearted way of looking at things, if you ask me." Mom planted her hands on her hips. "I think we've gone past the point of taking cookies to the neighbors. We need to dig deeper."

"What are you thinking?" I had my own idea.

Finishing Mrs. Lincoln's genealogy search topped my list. "I need to know first and last names of everyone who lives on this street."

"We're back to visiting on the pretense of the neighborhood watch."

"It isn't a pretense. I'm serious. If more folks were patrolling the neighborhood, then maybe Torie would still be alive."

"There's your opening. Go door-to-door and ask for names and phone numbers for emergency purposes, but I think we probably already have that information. Between the two of us and our suspect list, we can fill in the blanks." She led the way to the house.

She headed for the kitchen and I headed upstairs for my laptop. I unplugged it and carried it to the kitchen table. Time to get into research mode.

Mom set out the makings of sandwiches and glasses of lemonade as I plugged in my laptop. She slid the notepad containing our notes in my direction. "We need Mrs. Henley's first name. We know the Olsons and the Edgars, and poor Torie's. Is there anyone else?"

I studied the list and added Sarah and Ben Thompson, then pulled up Google maps and researched Mrs. Henley's address. Bingo. "Mrs. Henley's name is Marilyn." Now who allowed their name to be found so easy? I needed to make sure my location would be harder to find. The last thing I needed was avid fans knocking on my door.

The introvert neighbors, the Edgars, were harder to find. In fact, I couldn't find them anywhere on the web. I found lots of Edgars, just not those with the names of Herman and Cecilia. I drummed my fingers on the table, then typed their address into Google and found a satellite image of their house, but still no name. Next, I typed their name and their address. Hmmm. The listing showed a management company as the owner, but when I purchased my property, I was told there were no rentals in the neighborhood.

I glanced in the direction of their house, wishing I could see through walls. Even with the doors and windows closed, I heard the sound of a wood chipper. "I really wish we could peek around inside the Edgars' house. I can't find them anywhere on the internet. It's as if they don't exist."

"Why can't we?" Mom slid a paper plate containing a ham and cheese sandwich toward me.

"Other than the fact that trespassing is against the law, those people scare me."

"Why? Because they're unfriendly? That isn't a crime. They stick to themselves, also not a crime, but I happen to know," Mom waved a potato chip. "That they go somewhere every Friday night. I suspect it's Bingo at the Catholic Church."

Tomorrow was Friday. Did we dare? I stared at a cobweb in the corner of the kitchen that Mom had missed during her weekly cleaning. Maybe I was wrong in my assumption. Just because my neighbors were private people, didn't make them murderers. Rusty was still the most likely suspect, but my gut told me he was innocent.

"Have you read that woman's manuscript yet?"

Mom's question pulled me back to the table. "No. I don't plan on it."

"Well, she's one sick puppy, I gotta tell you."
Mom shook her head. "The ways the characters die
in her story makes your stomach churn."

"Really?" Maybe the wannabe author is the
killer. It wasn't totally unheard of for an author to
take research a bit too far. Look at me ... solving a
crime just for the sake of injecting new passion into
my writing.

"Yep. Twisted. We should take a closer look at
her."

I typed Sarah Thompson into Google. Scores of
links came up: her website, a few self-published
titles on Amazon, and her Facebook page, to name a
few. I clicked on Facebook. Good, her profile was
public. Most of her entries were on the joys and
despairs of writing, but one post jumped out at me.
She mentioned how she needed to up her research
on what it felt like to kill someone.

I straightened in my chair. For the sake of the
community, and the purpose of finding a killer, I
might have to change one of my hard and fast rules.
I needed to meet with a wannabe author. Well, she
was an author, since she had several books on
eBook, but we'd play her game of wanting to find a
traditional publisher. "Where's the manuscript?"

"In my room. I'll be right back." Mom dashed
away, returning minutes later with a thick stack of
copy printed paper. "Don't read after you've eaten."

"Thanks for the warning." I shoved aside the
uneaten sandwich and dug into the darkest story I'd
ever read. Horror didn't begin to describe the
carnage of a family of cannibals. Who were the
Thompsons? The idea of meeting Sarah anywhere

other than a public place scared the bejeebers out of me. I fished in the tapestry bag for her business card and reached for the phone.

After many excited shrieks that almost burst my eardrum, she agreed to meet me at the coffee shop ten minutes away. We would meet in thirty minutes.

"Want me to go?" Mom asked. "I could sit unobtrusively in a corner and make sure she didn't put poison in your Starbucks."

"Poison seems a bit tame for these people." I shuddered. "I don't need to read the entire manuscript to realize it's too … much for a traditional publisher. I doubt she'll stab me with a straw at the coffee house."

"You never know." Mom shrugged. "If you aren't home by suppertime, I'll be contacting Matt to go looking for you. Do. Not. Leave. The coffee shop with her."

"Yes, mother." Most of the time it rankled when she treated me like a child, but this wasn't one of those times. Me, scaredy-cat Stormi Nelson was meeting a potential murderer. The thought caused sweat to trickle between my shoulder blades.

I ate the sandwich and drank the lemonade, despite the vivid images running through my mind like an out of control movie reel. I hadn't seen Mrs. Lincoln, but I could fill in the blanks. I did see Torie, and it would haunt me forever. Now, I had the few lines I'd read of Sarah's book churning in my mind as well.

She had moved to the top of my suspect list. Only problem was, how did I go about asking someone how far she would actually go for research? Should I just blurt out the question of whether or not she would kill for the sake of her story?

16

Sarah Thompson, hair freshly dyed a crow's black, and red-blood lipstick on her full lips, looked like a plump vampire as she waved from a corner table at the local bookstore and Starbucks. I returned her wave with a smile I hoped wasn't a grimace and made my way to her.

I set the manuscript on the table, preferring to get right to the point. No time for idle chit-chat.

"Here. I read on your website that you like mocha frozen coffee drinks, so I bought you one." Sarah grinned, showing a streak of lipstick on her teeth.

I rubbed my forefinger over my teeth, hoping she'd take the hint. We couldn't have a serious conversation when she looked as if she'd just sucked blood from her latest victim and I wasn't confident enough to point out another person's faults. At least not verbally.

She got the hint and scrubbed her teeth with a napkin. "How do you like my new look?" She set the napkin down and patted her hair. "It makes me look exotic, don't you think? Maybe a little sultry? I've even started wearing lower cut blouses."

Yeah, I'd noticed that. Her cleavage threatened to suffocate both of us. "It's very ... romance author like." If you wrote erotica, which she did, along with a whole other mess of stuff.

She beamed. "What did you think of the story?"

The dreaded question now hung in the air. I took a sip of my drink to stall. How could I tactfully tell her that her story sucked, that she needs to learn the craft better, but not to stop writing?

"You hated it." Her face fell while her eyes hardened.

"I didn't say that. I do think it's a bit ... much for most readers." I picked at the napkin under my cup. "Have you ever considered attending a writer's conference in order to improve your writing? It would help tremendously and give you the opportunity to meet editors and agents face-to-face." A small pile of shredded white paper grew beside the cup.

"Your writing is so gritty. How do you do your research?" There. It was out. I sat back and focused on her face.

"I'll do almost anything for a story." She sat back and crossed her arms. She laughed. "Do you actually think I've killed someone and eaten them? Oh, this is funny. Surely you know research can be done by reading what others have done before you."

"Of course I do. You write with ... a lot of description." I shuddered. "Maybe tone it back a bit. Let the reader fill in some of the blanks."

"I think there's a market out there for this style of story."

"I agree, but you may have to self-publish."

Hmmm. Maybe she wasn't the killer after all, but I wasn't ready to put a line through her name on my suspect list quite yet.

"Maybe I will." She grabbed the bag containing her manuscript. "Thanks for nothing. I thought with how nice and friendly you seemed on your website that you would be willing to help a new author." She stood. "I was wrong." With a flick of her inky hair, she stormed from the store.

I sighed and followed her outside, just as she stabbed a pocket knife into one of my tires. "Hey!"

She tossed me a wave and jumped into a Volkswagen Bug convertible before speeding away. She gave three honks and raced out of sight.

I dug my cell phone out of my purse and dialed Matt's number. "Detective Steele."

"Matt, it's Stormi. I just watched Sarah Thompson stick a knife into my tire."

"Where are you?"

"I'm at the coffee shop inside Books and More." My hand trembled, whether from fear or anger I wasn't sure. I'd never had someone mad enough at me to retaliate with violence.

"I'm on my way."

I sat on a bench outside the store and waited. It took Matt ten minutes to show up. He pulled beside my Mercedes and got out of his dark, government-issued sedan. My mouth watered. I thought he looked good in jeans. He was fabulous in dress slacks, shirt and tie, hair slicked back and dark sunglasses covering his eyes. He strolled toward me with long strides.

"What did you do?"

Okay, he lost some of his fabulousness. "Why do you assume I did anything?"

"You must have provoked her." He held up a hand when I started to protest. "I'm not saying what she did was right, I'm trying to gather the facts."

"I told her she needed to improve her writing craft. You should read the sick and twisted stuff she writes."

He nodded and marched back to my car, leaving me to follow, which I did. "I'll change the flat and go talk to her. Do you want to file a complaint?"

"No, but I do want her to pay for the new tire and not to come within fifty feet of me."

"File a restraining order. I doubt you'll get any money from her unless it goes to court, and the cost of a tire doesn't really justify court." He rubbed his chin. "Try not to antagonize her any further, okay?"

"Definitely." I watched as he changed the tire. "I think she might be our killer."

He wiped his hands on a rag I had in my trunk. "Why do you say that?"

"She had a lot of detail in her books on gruesome murders and flat out told me she'd do almost anything for a story."

"Key word being almost. That isn't the same as killing for research." He tossed the rag back into the trunk along with the jack and the flat tire. "Stay away from her. We're checking into all your neighbors, Stormi, but none of them are higher on our list than the others."

"Did you know that there is no record of the Edgars online? It's like they don't exist. Don't you find that strange?" I jogged around the car after him as he headed back to his sedan.

"They're private people." He opened his car door. "Look, I understand your fascination with this case, but again, I'm asking you to leave it alone. I'll talk to you later." He slid into his car and drove away, leaving me feeling ten times the fool for sharing what little information I had.

I'd show him and the rest of the police department. I could catch this killer and protect my family at the same time. The consequences of possible failure were too horrible to contemplate. I drove home with my blood boiling at Sarah and disappointment in Matt.

It wasn't until I got home that I realized I'd forgotten all about getting a restraining order. Since I was no longer in the mood to go anywhere, I headed to my office to squeeze in some more writing and maybe a bit of research on the genealogy of the neighbors. Bless my mother, she'd put my laptop back on my desk.

I debated about whether or not to have a character like Sarah in my story. After all, she might read my books, although I doubted it since she thought I wrote the same type of books she did. If I put her in my book, she would obviously recognize herself and possibly take offense. But, her character would be as colorful as she was and make the story interesting. I kept her in my plot.

The delicious aroma of chocolate cake wafted up the stairs and under my office door. Since I wasn't Super Woman who could ignore such a call, I saved my work and headed to the kitchen.

Mom was just taking a cake out of the oven.

"Look what I'm taking to the Edgars household. I've made a lemon cake for the Thompsons … what?"

I explained the result of my meeting with Sarah. "I'm not sure she'll be welcoming toward what she might consider a peace offering."

"Oh, pooh. You do have a way of spoiling my plans." Mom set the cake on the counter. "Well, maybe I can get her to conspire with me against you. If she thinks I loved her book and you didn't, she might talk to me."

I liked the idea, but not the idea of Mom going over there alone. "It's too dangerous."

"I'll have my Taser." She set up the ingredients for homemade frosting. "You go back upstairs and do whatever it is you do. I've got this. Oh, you might want to check on Rusty. He's supposed to be trimming the tree in the backyard, but I haven't heard any sound of a trimmer in almost an hour. I hope he didn't cut his leg off."

I grabbed a water bottle from the fridge before pushing out the back door. Only the sounds of birds and the Edgars' wood chipper greeted me. What did they possibly find to chop up so often? If they were making their own mulch, they probably had enough for the entire neighborhood by now.

The limb trimmer lay on the ground, unplugged from the electrical socket. "Rusty?" Maybe he had gone into the woods at the back of the house. I'd paid extra to buy the house with a wooded area and hiking trails behind it. Since the land wasn't zoned residential, I'd never have to worry about neighbors to the back of me.

A creek ran through the property and happily flowed along beside the trail. Still no sign of my gardener. I glanced at my watch. Lunchtime. He could have gone home for a bite to eat, although Mom made sure to feed him each day. Where could that man be?

I headed back to the yard and picked up the trimmers. I definitely didn't want to leave them in the yard for someone to steal. Sadie barked along the fence line, her head through a hole in the fence behind one of my flowering rose bushes. "Here, girl!" If she irritated the neighbors too much, they might take matters into their own hands and I'd be minus a dog.

I knelt and grabbed her collar, my gaze falling on something red on the grass. Was that blood? I stood and followed the trail of drops along the fence and into the forest. The trail stopped at the Edgars' back gate. Rusty! I knew his peeping would get him in trouble. I snapped my fingers for Sadie to follow me and dashed back to the house.

I slammed through the door, locking it behind me. "I think the Edgars killed Rusty."

"What are you talking about?" Mom spun, the frosting covered spatula in her hand falling to the floor.

"I found a blood trail and it led right to their back fence. Our limb trimmer was left on the ground. Rusty is always careful to put away the tools."

"Heavens." Mom clasped her hands to her chest. "Do you really think they did away with him?"

"I don't know what to think, but I really need to

see inside their backyard."

"Go to the attic. You can see perfectly from there."

"You know this from experience?"

"Of course, I do. I've found ways to spy on all of our neighbors."

We thundered up the stairs and into the stifling heat of the attic. Mom opened the wood slats covering a port-hole type window that looked down into the yard of the Edgars' house.

Herman dragged a large black lawn and leaf bag across the yard. The bulges in the bag looked suspiciously like what could be a human body cut into pieces. Could a person kill and cut up another person in an hour?

Mom clutched my hand as Herman pulled out a leg and handed it to Cecelia. She shoved it into the chipper.

Mom fainted.

17

I was torn between watching the grisly scene in the neighbor's yard and checking on Mom. Just as I'd made my decision to see if Mom was all right, she sat up.

"I've got binoculars in my room." She got to her feet and dashed off, returning minutes later with a pair of binoculars still in the box. She thrust them into my hands. "Here. I can't bear to look."

I almost asked when she had bought them, but instead tore into the package like a Christmas gift then trained them on the wood chipper. "I see something red on the ground around the chipper." Nausea rose in me. Oh. My. Gosh. They had chopped up Rusty and were turning him into mulch. "Call Matt. Hurry! My cell phone is in my pocket."

She almost pulled me off my feet trying to retrieve the device. Her hands shook so bad it took much longer than necessary. I retrained the binoculars back on the chipper. "Now, they're shoving in an arm."

"Mercy." She punched in Matt's number. "The Edgars are shoving Rusty's body parts into a wood chipper ... It's Ann Nelson. For crying out loud, we saw you just the other day. We need you!" She hung up. "He'll come. What are they doing now? How are they going to shove in the torso ... or the head?"

"Mom, stop. You're grossing me out." I didn't see any more parts going into the chipper, thank goodness. I sagged against the wall. "They're done."

Poor Rusty. Tears stung my eyes. Poor simple-minded fool. I always knew his Peeping Tom habits would get him killed. Wait. This meant the Edgars were our killers.

The doorbell rang, and Mom and I pushed and shoved to get out of the attic and downstairs. "It's my house."

"I live here, too." She elbowed me in the ribs, knocking the breath from my lungs, before yanking open the door. She reached out, grabbed Matt's arm, and dragged him inside.

His eyes widened as he glanced from her to me. "What in the world is going on here? Stormi, you first."

"I went looking for Rusty because we didn't hear any lawn equipment for about an hour. I found the trimmer on the ground, unusual for him, and followed blood spots through the fence to the Edgars' yard. Then, we saw them shoving body parts into the wood chipper." I shuddered. "There's blood on the ground all around the chipper. They are the killers."

"Don't jump to conclusions. There could be a simple explanation."

"For body parts in a wood chipper? Seriously?

I'd like to hear that explanation. It would make a best-selling story." I crossed my arms and glared. "I'll be sure to use it in one of my books."

"Don't be angry. I'll go check it out and let you know what I find. Stay in your house." He left and, with one hand on the gun at his waist, marched to the Edgars' house.

Mom and I stayed on our own property, but stepped outside and moved as far across the lawn as we could and still be on our property. We hid behind the rhododendron bush.

Matt rang the doorbell. I counted to ten before the door swung open, and he stepped back. I couldn't hear what was being said, but soon Matt stepped off the porch and moved to the back of the house, entering through a side gate. Mom and I moved to our backyard and peered through holes in the fence.

"Keep your finger pressed on the emergency button on your phone," Mom whispered. "I don't put it past them not to bash Matt in the head and add him to Rusty's remains."

"Shhh." I had a firm grip on my cell phone.

Matt peered into the wood chipper, then looked into the black bag at his feet. He shook his head and glanced our way. I could see the movement of his shoulders as he sighed deeply. What lie had they told him?

We ran through the back door and waited for Matt in the front room. He entered without knocking. "It's squirrel blood. They kill squirrels when they won't stay out of their bird feeder." He raised a hand at our protests. "I told them it was against the law, and they promised not to do it again. As for the body … it's a mannequin. They're cleaning out the attic in that old house and rather than crowd the landfill, they chop things up in some effort to help the environment."

"Then where is Rusty?" I lifted my chin. "I seriously doubt the blood trail in my backyard is from a rodent."

"Show me."

I led him to the backyard and showed him the drops of blood. He made a call asking for forensics to come out and take an analysis, then hung up and turned to me. "I'm sure Rusty will show up. He's a wanderer."

"He's never left without finishing his work." I glanced toward the Edgars' house. "He eats his meals with us and doesn't go home until dark. Something is wrong. I feel it in my gut."

"Are you sure it isn't your over-active writer's imagination brought on by the episode this morning?" He tucked a strand of hair that had fallen from my ponytail behind my ear.

"I'm positive." I stepped back out of his reach. If he couldn't take me more seriously, then he had no right to make tender gestures toward me.

Hurt clouded his eyes. "I'll call you later. Forensics should be here within the hour." He whirled and marched away, his shoulders slumped.

My heart lurched a bit, knowing I'd hurt his feelings, but he had also hurt mine. There was something wrong with Rusty's disappearance whether the Edgars played a part or not, and I didn't like having my intuitions brushed aside as if they weren't important.

Voices from the other side of the fence, prompted me to put an eye to a peep hole in the wood slats. Herman gestured wildly, his wife's gaze darting toward our house. She shook her head and marched away. What I wouldn't have given for a device that allowed me to hear over a longer distance.

"I'm sure they know if it was us that called Matt," Mom said beside me. "If they are the killers, then we're in more danger than before."

"If Matt thought they killed Mrs. Lincoln and Torie, he wouldn't leave us alone." I hoped. At the very least, he would assign an officer to sit outside our house, right? "Which cake did you make for the Edgars?"

"The lemon one."

"I think it's time for me to deliver it with an apology." I straightened. I didn't know what I would say, but I was a writer. I worked with words every day. Surely, I could come up with something plausible to say.

"I'll need to frost it real quick." Mom raced into the house.

Fifteen minutes later, I rang the Edgars' doorbell and waited. This time I counted to ten before the curtains twitched, then another ten before Cecelia answered the door. I plastered a smile to my face, knowing Mom watched closely from our yard.

"Well, if it isn't the residential nosey neighbor." Cecelia crossed her arms across her bony chest. "Can't you stay to yourself and mind your own business? Now, we'll most likely be fined for killing rodents."

"I'm sorry. My mother has a tendency to jump to conclusions." I inwardly apologized for throwing Mom under the bus. "We've brought you a cake for the inconvenience."

She snorted and took the cake, then slammed the door in my face. I'd accomplished nothing. Spirits low, and still worried about Rusty, I headed home and told Mom what I'd done.

Instead of getting angry, she agreed I'd done the best thing. "We can't have all the neighbors mad at the same person, now can we? This way, maybe they'll be more willing to talk to you, like Mrs. Henley is with me."

I doubted it, but slung an arm around her shoulders and gave her a hug. "You're the best. I don't deserve you." I turned as Angela pulled into the driveway. She was home early.

After turning off the ignition and exiting her car, she marched toward us. "Can you stay out of trouble for one day? I swear, you're all the station is talking about. Our family is nothing but a big joke. It's embarrassing. Can't you tell a real body from a dummy?"

I bit my tongue rather than spouting off that I was looking at the world's biggest dummy at that moment. "It was an honest mistake."

"Whatever. I was so mortified, I pretended to be sick and came home early. I'm taking a bath and holing up in my room. Where are the kids?"

Mom and I shrugged.

Angela huffed. "I can't even rely on my family to watch my children."

"Were we supposed to?" Mom asked. "They're either in their room or roaming the streets as usual. I wasn't aware you'd enforced any rules for them. They know where home is and what time to eat. Other than that, your sweet darlings avoid us like the plague."

Angela stormed into the house. Seconds later, her screeches reached us as she shouted at her little darlings for still being in bed.

"She needs to find something for them to do during the summer," Mom said. "It isn't good for them to sleep so much."

"I think they stay up all night playing video games." With one more glance toward the Edgars house, I followed Mom inside ours.

Angela screamed for a few more minutes before slamming the bathroom door.

"Is she gone?" Cheyenne opened her door a crack.

"You're safe."

"Good." Cheyenne stepped out of her room wearing the shortest shorts I'd ever seen and a tube top. "I'm going out. I'll be home by supper."

My mouth fell open. "Aren't you getting dressed first?"

"I am dressed. A group of us are going to the lake." She banged on Dakota's door on her way. Soon, he followed wearing board shorts and a tank top.

It wasn't my place to tell them to ask for permission. At least we knew where they were going and the approximate time they would return. Still, I would suggest to my sister, once she was speaking to me again, that she put a GPS on their phones.

I headed for my office and closed the door. I didn't have as good of a vantage point for keeping surveillance on Herman and Cecelia from there, but could see most of their property and still keep an eye on the road and several of the neighbors. My gut told me there was more to Rusty's disappearance than him simply wandering off for a while. Maybe it was an innocent reason, but I couldn't rest easy until I knew more.

A door slammed across the street. Mrs. Henley dashed off her porch and into her van. The garage door rose, she drove in, the door closed, and two minutes later, the door rose again and she backed out. Only this time, there was a slumped over figure in the front seat.

It was hard to tell whether the second person was Rusty or not. Either way, they didn't look conscious. I reached for my cell phone to call Matt, then thought better of it. After all, I had no grounds on which to call him. It wasn't against the law for someone to park outside their garage then drive inside to pick up a passenger, only suspicious.

Why couldn't I have normal neighbors like everyone else in the world? I shifted my gaze east. Herman stood in his driveway and watched as Mrs. Henley drove away. Once her van was out of sight, he tossed the cake I'd dropped off into the trash receptacle on the curb.

18

Later that evening, I sat on the porch swing, laptop on my lap and stared at the genealogy charts I'd made of my neighbors. This was where I knew the answers to so many questions laid. The fact that I couldn't find a single thing on the Edgars irritated me like a tick embedded in a hard to reach place.

Not to mention how much it rankled that they threw away the cake Mom baked without taking a single bite. Maybe they thought we had poisoned it?

Mary Ann raced up the sidewalk, leaped up the steps, and landed with a plop on the seat next to me. "Guess what?"

"What?"

"Rusty has disappeared. Sources say his mother is hiding him."

I prayed that was the truth. We'd know better once Matt got the results of the blood analysis. "Who are your sources?"

"My ears, when my brother is talking on the phone to his police buddies." Her teeth flashed in the moonlight. "I'm a great eavesdropper."

"I guess you heard how I made a fool of myself." I closed my laptop.

She giggled. "It's all over the precinct how you're not only a nosey neighbor romance writer, but prone to vivid acts of imagination. The Edgars have filed a complaint against you."

"Good for them." I sighed and leaned back in the swing, setting it into motion with my toe. "Something about them bothers me. Like, who are they? I can't find any record of a Herman and Cecelia Edgars."

"Leave them alone." Matt hopped over the railing and booted his sister off the swing so he could take the space next to me. He moved my laptop to a small wicker table beside the swing. "Are you still mad at me?"

"I'm not mad at you." I scooted over a fraction of an inch.

He laughed, startling bats from the magnolia tree in our front yard. Mary Ann shrieked and ran into the house. "If I knew that was how to get rid of my sister, I would have tried it a long time ago," he said. "Little sisters can be a pest when big brother wants to spend time with a pretty woman."

"Flattery will get you nowhere." In fact, it would get him everywhere. I scooted back to his side and snuggled under his arm. "I was never mad at you. But something fishy is going on in Oak Meadow."

"We're in agreement on that." He rested his cheek against my hair. "I can't tell you anything more than to stop antagonizing your neighbors before you put yourself in danger. I'm on it. Trust me."

I wanted to, I really did. But I had gotten myself

so deep in an effort to write a new book, that I really wanted to see how it all ended. Not that I wanted to be foolish and endanger myself. Maybe I could work behind the scenes, so to speak, and do my investigating on my laptop instead of pounding the pavement. "Mom will be very disappointed."

"So will my sister, and they will both be fine."

"What reason could there be for someone to be invisible on the internet? I've tried searching for them and they have no online footprint at all."

"Stormi." His sigh raised my head and inch, then lowered it with his exhale.

"It's for research."

"Sure it is." He shifted on the swing. "Hypothetically, they could have changed their names for any number of reasons, but mainly in order to hide."

What reason would the Edgars' have to hide? Maybe they were in the Witness Protection Program. I fought against the urge to straighten. Being a novelist, I was also an avid reader and this new thought wasn't totally out of left field. In fact, it held more merit than any other point I could come with. The problem now was, how could I find out? I couldn't exactly march into the FBI headquarters and demand an explanation about my unfriendly neighbors.

"I can hear the wheels turning in your head." Matt tilted my face up to his. "What are you thinking?"

"That the Edgars are in the Witness Protection Program." His stiffening told me all I needed to know. I grinned and scooted against the opposite end of the swing so I could see his face better. "Don't worry. I won't say a thing." But … they must have tipped off someone very dangerous to want to hide in Oak Meadow Estates. I resisted the urge to rub my hands together. Somehow, they were connected to the deaths of Mrs. Lincoln and Torie.

What if those they were hiding from had found them and the murders were meant as a warning? If so, why not go straight to the Edgars? Why kill innocent people? It had to be something else. Oh. I jerked upright. "They know something and those after them can't kill them until they get the information."

"What are you talking about?" The full moon gave enough illumination for me to see his frown.

"It's for my book." Which wasn't exactly a lie.

"You're digging into dangerous territory, Stormi." He stood. "I don't think we should see each other until this case is over. I've already said too much. Anything more and you and your family will be in harm's way." He left a kiss on my forehead, branding his lips on my skin, then left.

What just happened? The summer evening took on a definite chill. I wrapped my arms around my middle as Matt strolled down the sidewalk and out of sight. Tears stung my eyes. Why couldn't I keep my mouth shut? He had told me to stay out of things, and whether I intended to or not, I didn't have to push the issue. I felt a little better reminding myself he only said until the case was over, but what if he forgot how hot things ran between us? Maybe the old adage of absence makes the heart grow fonder wasn't really true.

A loud bang from next door startled me out of my musing. I glanced through my front window to see Mom and Mary Ann flipping through sheets of paper. My Taser lay on the coffee table in front of them. If the Edgars had filed a complaint against me, I couldn't very well climb through the shrubs and go nosing around, could I? Unless I didn't get caught. I bit my bottom lip. No, it would have to be someone else.

"Mom?" I pushed open the front door. "Where are the cats?"

"Under the table where they always are, why?" She cocked her head. "What are you planning?"

I scooped Ebony into my arms and kissed his dark face. "You're going to help Momma, aren't you?" I glanced at Mom and Mary Ann. "One of you will have to go after him, and maybe catch a peek through the window of the house next door and report back what you find."

"You're going to sacrifice your cat for a story?" Mary Ann looked aghast. "That's brilliant."

"I'm not sacrificing him." For goodness sake. What kind of person did she think I was? "We'll leave the back door open. He never wanders far. The poor thing hates the outdoors, but the neighbor doesn't know that now do they?"

"Oh, daughter, you have a wicked mind. I'll do it. You're not allowed over there." Mom grabbed the cat from me. "My Taser is in my pocket, and I'm ready to go."

Suddenly my plan seemed like a very bad idea. "Don't get caught, okay?"

"I'll do my best. If I get arrested, you're going

down with me" She cooed to my cat and scuttled out the front door. Mary Ann and I followed as far as the front porch.

Ebony tried to scoot past us, but Mary Ann firmly closed the door. He meowed and shot around the corner of the house. "I'll get the back door," Mary Ann said.

Soon, she had rejoined me and Mom's loud whispers of "Here, kitty kitty," rang through the neighborhood. Her voice got softer the closer she got to the Edgars' kitchen window.

"Ebony is already safely in the house," Mary Ann said. "You know your animals well."

Yes, I did. I also knew enough not to let Sadie out. Her whines and scratches at the door told me how unpleased she was. Not that she would be much of a deterrent to anyone wanting to harm me, but she usually made more noise than Mom and I combined.

"I can't see Mom." I leaned over the banister, trying to peer through the hedge separating the two properties. I meowed, hoping to draw her back into view.

"That's the worst impression of a cat I've ever heard." She popped her head over the bushes. "Quiet down."

I shrieked and fell headfirst over the railing into a tangle of arms, legs, and scratchy branches. When I tried to crawl out, my hair entangled with a leafy branch, imprisoning me. "Mary Ann," I hissed. "I'm stuck."

"What?" She leaned over in the same place I had fallen.

"Be careful. I fell and can't get out."

She giggled. "Want me to call Matt?"

"No." I cried, knowing coming to rescue me was the last thing he wanted to do. "Come help me."

She climbed over the railing, as nimble as a monkey, and crawled to my side. "Hold still. You're really in a bind."

I thought she was going to pull my hair out by the roots. "Ow!"

"Shhh." She soon had me free and back on my feet. "You make enough noise to scare away a bear."

Mom made her way to our side. "They're dragging stuff from the attic into the living room. I couldn't see anything through the kitchen window, so I moved to their porch. I didn't see the cake I baked them anywhere."

Oops. "They threw it away."

"What?!"

I clamped my hand over her mouth. "They'll hear you."

"I don't care. I want my plate back." She yanked free and marched to their front door.

Mary Ann put her arms around me. "What do we do if they drag her inside?"

"Then, we'll call your brother." Upset with me or not, Matt wouldn't say no to saving my mother.

The front door opened after Mom banged several times. I couldn't hear what was said, but knew from Mom's hand gestures and arm waving that she was giving them a piece of her mind.

Herman stepped off the porch and marched to

the trash can. He fished inside and came out with Mom's plate. On his way back, he spotted us in the bushes. He shook his head and handed the plate to Mom then slammed the door after him.

"That man is a killer if I ever met one." Mom stormed past us, into the house, and into the kitchen. "I almost wanted him to make a move on me so I could shock him with my Taser." She glanced at my scratched arms. "What happened to you?"

"I fell in the bushes."

"Of course, you did." She set her dish in the sink and collapsed into a kitchen chair.

"I could help y'all, you know, but obviously I'm not invited into this prestigious group of yours." Angela came out of the pantry, a chocolate bar in her hand. "I do work at the police station where I'm privy to all sorts of information."

"I didn't know you wanted to help." I pulled out a chair. As the younger sister, I'd never felt like anything but a nuisance to my popular older sister.

"Of course I do. You never asked me." She joined us at the table, licking the chocolate off her fingers. "What do you want me to find out? One of the officers has a thing for me. I'm sure with a little encouragement, he'll tell me anything I want to know." She leaned her elbows on the table and gave me a Cheshire cat smile. "Like why the Edgars are in the Witness Protection."

"They are?"

"Yep. I snooped on your laptop, saw what you were researching, and put two and two together, then asked some questions. I'm not stupid, you know, and I'm willing to ask more questions, with the proper motivation, of course."

"What type of motivation?" I crossed my arms.

"That you let me stay here, indefinitely, until I decide I'm ready to move. Where else can I afford a place like this?"

I thrust my hand toward her. "It's a deal."

What kind of new horror had I just unleashed by being indebted to Angela?

19

After a week of no new clues or any contact with Matt, life drifted along in a haze. While I caught up on my writing, now half-way through my first mystery, I could go no further until I knew the identity of the murderer.

The Edgars stayed to themselves and Mrs. Henley hadn't returned home after her suspicious departure. I clipped the leash on Sadie's collar. A walk would do both of us some good and hopefully release some of my nervous energy.

"Hey, Aunt Stormi." Dakota stuck his head out of his room. "Can you come here?"

I followed him into his room. He shut the door and pulled the blinds. "I've been doing some more investigating, there's nothing else to do around here, and I've stumbled across something you might find interesting." He lifted the lid on his laptop. "Did you know your Mrs. Henley did some time for assault?"

"What?" I dropped Sadie's leash and stared at the computer screen. Sure enough, five years ago she served three months in the county jail for bashing a woman over the head with a shovel. The victim allegedly called her son a retard. Hmmm. Very interesting. "Good work, Dakota."

He grinned. "I've been doing some … spying, don't tell Mom, and Mrs. Henley has left her backdoor unlocked. Wanna take a look inside?"

Did I? We'd be breaking so many laws by taking a look inside, but Mrs. Henley had been gone for a while with no word to anyone. Maybe she was in danger. If so, it was my duty as the head of the Neighborhood Watch to check it out, right? Plus, it wasn't safe to leave a house unlocked, even in Oak Meadow Estates.

"I should probably go alone. I wouldn't want you to get into trouble."

He frowned. "Haven't I proven that I'm a good detective?" His hurt expression was my undoing.

"Fine, but you'll stay outside as lookout." No sense in both of us getting arrested for entering uninvited.

"Whatever." He grabbed Sadie's leash and stormed from his room, banging the door against the wall.

Teenagers. I shrugged and followed. While Sadie always walked sedately by my side on walks, she pranced and twirled and yipped when Dakota held the leash. It might have something to do with him playing along with her. I smiled. I really needed to spend more time with my niece and nephew … without breaking the law in order to do so.

"We'll go through the alley." Dakota ducked through a loose board behind a vacant house for sale.

I glanced both ways and squeezed through after him. Soon, we stared at the back of Mrs. Henley's house. A curtain blew from a window over the garage where Rusty lived. The Henley's sure were trusting people, and Dakota and I were about to violate that trust.

My heart leaped into my throat. I squelched down my guilt and reservations while pushing open the back door to the kitchen. "Hello?" Not that I expected anyone to answer, but I didn't want to get shot or bashed in the head. Especially if the owner had a prior record. "Mrs. Henley?" I looped Sadie's leash over a handrail on the back steps.

"They're not here." Dakota shook his head. "But … there is a van in the garage. Does she own more than one?"

"I don't know." Very curious.

The cloying scent of too much vanilla incense hung over the musty smell of a house closed up for a week. I stepped into a kitchen that looked unlived in. No dirty dishes in the sink, a table set for company, curtains with sharp creases hanging over the sink, and vacuum tracks in the carpet. If we walked across it, we'd leave tracks for sure.

Dakota and I stared at the carpet. "Oh, well." He marched across it and to a closet next to the front door. "Here's the vacuum. We'll make as little footprints as necessary then vacuum on our way out."

"Then how are we going to get back across?" Who was this kid?

He yanked open a drawer and pulled out a dishtowel. "We'll step on this as we vacuum."

I had a bad feeling about our plan. But, curiosity won out. I headed for the garage.

Sure enough, a slate-gray colored van sat inside. What had been the color of the one she had driven off in a week ago? It had looked dark. Maybe I could have Angela check DMV records to see whether Mrs. Henley owned two. I closed the door and surveyed the kitchen, doubting very much I'd find anything of interest.

"Found the office!"

I cringed at Dakota's shout. If he wanted to be a detective, he'd have to be a bit quieter about it. If we got caught, Angela would kill me, and Mom would be mad because we hadn't invited her along.

Heading down the hall, walking as softly as I could, I glanced in doors as I went. Every room, bathroom, bedroom, they all looked as if they had recently been cleaned. Except for the fine film of dust over the surfaces. If Mrs. Henley had come home any time in the last week, I couldn't imagine her not dusting. While I loved my three-story Victorian, her cottage-style home was quaint and decorated like the inside of a magazine. I admitted to a small amount of jealousy.

"I got nothin'," Dakota said. "No computer, no file cabinet, nada. But …" he pointed at a square patch on the carpet. "I think a cabinet sat there."

Why would she leave and take her filing cabinet? "Let's cover our tracks and check out Rusty's apartment." I grabbed the vacuum, cleared our tracks, then walked across the trail of dish towels, picking them up as I went. Should I put them in the hamper in the laundry room or fold them and place back in the drawer? I doubted Mrs. Henley would want to use them after I'd walked on them. I tossed them in the full hamper.

Back outside, we headed for the steep stairs on the side of the garage. Just like the house, the apartment door was unlocked. We stepped inside to a clean, sparsely furnished apartment. I froze two feet inside the door.

Plastered along one wall were photos of every person in the neighborhood as they went about their lives. I'd never noticed Rusty carrying a camera, but the evidence didn't lie. There were photos of Cheyenne and Dakota walking to school, me walking Sadie, even one of me taken through my office window as I worked on my book.

There were several of Mom puttering in the yard, a lot of the Edgarses in different rooms of their house. Several showed them with their heads together, deep in conversation in their backyard. There were some of Torie as she walked arm in arm with Bob. Those had a red line drawn through them, as did one of a woman whom I believed to be Mrs. Lincoln. She was planting flowers at the time the photo was taken.

I put a hand over my heart and stumbled backward. I couldn't believe Rusty was the killer. Why else would he have all these photos? I needed to let Matt know. An anonymous phone call should do the trick.

"Look." Dakota held up a pad of paper. "It looks like a child's writing, but there are notes on a bunch of people." With wide eyes, he handed me the pad.

One note in particular grabbed my attention and stole my breath. The bad man killed Torie. "If Rusty has all these photos, why doesn't he have one of the murder taking place?"

"Unless he did it," Dakota said. "He wouldn't take a selfie of him killing someone."

True. I tossed the pad on the table under the photos and rushed down the stairs. Grabbing Sadie's leash, I set off at a fast pace, leaving Dakota to catch up. I had no idea what to do with the information we had found. One … either Rusty was the killer or two … he knew who was and was either dead or had fled with his mother. I wanted to believe number two, but my brain spun faster than the spin cycle of my washing machine.

Once I was away from the house, I dug out my cell phone and called Angela. "I need you to see if you can find out whether Mrs. Henley owned two vehicles and what model and color they are?"

"What did you find?"

"Just do it, please. Also, see what you can dig up on Rusty Henley."

"I've already tried that. He doesn't have a record for anything more than trespassing."

I bit my bottom lip. I'd read enough novels to know that Rusty could be the bad man he was talking about. What if he suffered from a split personality? What if he actually was the killer but thought someone else had done the killing while he was nothing more than a witness. Of course, I could be on the wrong track and he was witness to an actual someone else committing the crimes.

"Let me know what you find out, okay? And,

Angela, be careful. I have a feeling the you-know-what is about to hit the fan." I disconnected the call and watched as Dakota dashed toward me, shoving something into his pocket.

"Mrs. Henley just pulled into the driveway, driving a dark gray van." He bent over to catch his breath. "No sign of Rusty."

"We need to get out of here." I set off down the alley as fast as possible with a dog who wanted to stop and sniff every rock and bush. Once back on the street, I crossed and forced myself to slow to a more sedate pace in case anyone was watching. There wasn't anything unusual about me walking my dog, but running … that would raise questions. I never ran—anywhere.

Mom met us inside the front door, hands on her hips, and a scowl on her face. "Where did you two go?"

"Snooping." Dakota grinned and raced up the stairs.

I dragged Mom away from the door and filled her in on the day's findings. "What do you think?" I asked when I'd finished.

She twisted her lips while she thought for a minute. "I don't think Rusty is capable of killing, multiple personality or not. But … I do believe he knows who the killer is."

"It was hard enough to get information out of him. It will be harder now since he's missing." I perched on the back of the sofa. "If his mother wanted to hide him, I doubt she'll answer any questions we might have about what he knows."

"You think she knows what he knows?"

I shrugged. "You seem to know everything I do."

"True." She tapped her forefinger against her lips. "Mothers have a sense about such things. Especially when their children are up to no good. Angela is going to have a fit if she finds out Dakota went snooping with you."

I nodded. "He volunteered. The boy is a genius at finding out information."

Mom glanced out the window. "Well, if you have questions for Mrs. Henley, now's your chance. She's headed over here and looks as mellow as a tornado."

20

I waited until the second ring of the doorbell, which set Sadie to barking, before I answered the door. "Mrs. Henley, welcome back."

Her eyes narrowed. "How did you know I was gone?"

"I uh, saw you leave. I was sitting on the front—"

She waved a hand to cut me off. "Doesn't matter. Since you're the nosiest neighbor around here, I want to know if you saw someone nosing around my place. It's evident someone was inside my house."

"Who besides you has a key?"

"No one in this neighborhood locks their backdoor. Don't you know that?" She tried to peer around me. "There is also a big pile of dog poo in my backyard. You have the biggest dog around. Have you been letting that monster run loose?"

"Of course not. She is never off her leash." How could I have missed Sadie's "business"?

"Where's that nephew of yours? Kids nowadays have no respect for privacy. I wouldn't put it past him and his friends to play around in a house when the owner is gone."

"Was it trashed?"

"No. Very little was out of place, but I know someone was inside." She crossed her arms and stared at me. "In fact, I found a long, red hair on my carpet."

The blood rushed from my head to my feet. "What are you insinuating, Mrs. Henley?"

"I'm insinuating nothing. I'm flat out telling you that I think you were in my house while I was gone, nosing around in my personal business."

"Where's Rusty? He hasn't finished the job I assigned him."

She took a deep breath. "He's gone away for a few days to my sister in Little Rock. You're working him to death."

"Is he all right?" I forced myself to look compassionate and concerned rather than frightened out of my flip-flops. "I found blood near the tool he was using."

"He's fine. The boy is as strong as an ox." She jabbed a finger into my chest. "Stay out of my business. If you try to hurt that boy, I'll make you pay. Mind you remember that. No one messes with my son." She whirled and stomped back across the street.

I sagged against the wall while Mom closed the door. "She found a hair."

"For goodness sakes, you can't be the only red-head in these parts, but you should have been more careful with the dog."

"Now what?"

"We call a Neighborhood Watch meeting and

basically call out the killer. It will put a target on our backs, but this needs to come to an end." Mom motioned for me to follow her into the kitchen. "We'll state on the flier that there will be home-baked goodies and that dinner will be provided. That will bring just about everyone. We can get rid of some of those casseroles, you've cooked."

"That should clean us out of the casseroles." Then, I'd have room in the freezer for more. "I'll come up with a flier and have them printed off. Let's do the meeting tomorrow night at six o'clock." Like Mom, I was tired of the waiting. We'd light a fire under the residents of Oak Meadow Estates and see what runs out of the flames.

Fifteen minutes later, I had a simple flier made up; twenty copies printed off, and sent Dakota out on his skateboard to take the signs to every pole around the neighborhood. I tried to split the chore between him and his sister, but Cheyenne was having none of it. She didn't skateboard, didn't ride a bike, and wouldn't dare think about strolling around with her brother. I told Dakota I would pay him twenty dollars and he was off as fast as his skateboard would go.

While Mom baked some cookies to go with the chocolate cake she never delivered, I checked the freezer. Three casseroles might be enough, but I decided to make a dish of oven baked spaghetti just in case. There was no harm in having too much food. People were friendlier when their bellies were full.

*

At six p.m. on the dot, I approached the podium in the subdivision's shared clubhouse, totally surprised that everyone I knew was there. The Edgarses were sitting in the third row on the left, Mrs. Henley in the front row opposite Mary Ann and a scowling Matt. The Thompsons, Sarah scowling at me, sat in the back row. Across the aisle from them were the Olson's. Mrs. Olson had a possessive hand on her husband's arm. There were also several people I had to meet.

The only one missing was Rusty. While I was somewhat relieved that his mother said he was visiting an aunt, I still wasn't convinced he was out of danger. I cleared my throat and waited for the murmurs to stop. I didn't have a clear idea of what I was going to say, only that I needed to make the killer think I knew more than I did. Since my mother, sister, and nephew now felt compelled to help me solve the murders, I feared more for their safety with each passing day.

"Thank you for coming. As head of the Neighborhood Watch program, I felt compelled to invite all of you here to address some concerns." I glanced at the notes in front of me. "We've had complaints of gunshots to scare off bats, trespassing on other people's property, dogs leaving packages in people's yards, and general nosiness into other people's affairs."

"Most of which are complaints against you!" Herman Edgars yelled out.

I chose to ignore his comment. "Also, since the murders of Mrs. Lincoln and Victoria Lanham, I felt it necessary to inform the residents of Oak

Meadows Estate that the police are doing their best to discover the killer and that those with secrets—" I fixed a stare on the Edgarses and Mrs. Henley, "Well, these secrets are about to be revealed because of the diligence of this watch program."

Matt's eyes widened, and he fixed a stern look on me. I glanced away. If anyone could decipher that I was bluffing, it would be him. "Now, secrets are okay, but when these secrets endanger fellow neighbors, they should be brought into the light of day." Again, I glanced at my suspects. "Taking photographs of other residents without permission is strictly prohibited." There could no longer be any doubt in Mrs. Henley's mind that it was I who had trespassed.

Her eyes narrowed. If looks could kill, I'd be bleeding to death on the floor from the daggers she shot in my direction.

"Forgive me if I've overstepped my boundaries, but I've done background checks on all the residents and there are holes that need to be filled in. There will be questionnaires passed out at the end of the meeting. Please fill these out in their entirety and return to me. There will also be a sign-up sheet for volunteers willing to take turns patrolling the neighborhood."

"I'm not doing any patrolling at night when there is a murderer running loose," Mrs. Olson said. "That's a job best left to the police."

"I agree." Sarah Thompson stood. "As an aspiring writer of crime dramas, I'm as interested in anyone about the identity of the killer, but I'm not going to put myself out there to be killed. If you know something about someone, it is your duty to come clean, Miss Nelson."

"Yes, Miss Nelson, please do tell us what you know," Matt said before setting his mouth into a firm line.

"I will inform the police of my findings within the next few days." There. That should be the match to the flame I needed. "Any more questions? No? Then meeting adjourned. Enjoy the food."

I stepped down from the podium only to find my arm firmly grasped by Matt and myself dragged from the room. "Slow down."

"What in the heck do you think you're doing?" He stopped in a small alcove away from the main hall. "Do you want to get yourself killed?"

"I'm trying to draw out the killer. I think this will work."

"Most likely you'll be dead in three days." He raked his fingers through his hair, leaving the wheat-colored strands standing up like stalks of grain. "Do I need to put you under house arrest?"

"That won't stop the guilty party from coming after me." I crossed my arms and set my jaw. "I have a big dog, a Taser, and a houseful of people. Once the killer shows up, we'll call you. You can be there in two minutes."

"Woman, you're killing me. Haven't you thought of your family at all?"

Tears pricked my eyes. "That's why I'm doing this. I made a stupid decision just to write a book and now it has gone too far for me to back out now."

"I give up." His shoulders slumped. "I'll assign

a police officer to sit outside your house until this is over."

I shook my head. "That will deter the killer."

"I'll have him in an unmarked car. Just, please, keep your mother from taking him food or it will be a dead giveaway."

I cringed at his choice of words. "Are you even close to catching this person?"

"I can't tell you that."

"That means no."

"It means I can't tell you." He rolled his neck on his shoulders. "I have a primary suspect, yes."

"Good. The case is almost solved. You're welcome." I turned to go.

He stepped in front of me to stop me. "Welcome for what?"

"Helping you." I flashed him a grin, blinked away the tears, and went back to the meeting room to mingle with my suspects.

Mary Ann rushed toward me. "You are the bravest person I've ever met. Everyone is talking about what you could possibly know about them. The Edgares are talking about moving and Mrs. Henley is mad enough to chew glass because you've been snooping in her house." She planted fists on her slim hips. "And you didn't call me to go with you, naughty girl. Sarah Thompson is fuming because she says you are determined to write a better book than her and that you are stealing all of her notes. Everyone is leaving the meeting, taking their food with them."

It seemed as if I set the whole neighborhood on edge, which was exactly what I had intended. Now,

I needed to warn Sarah from saying too much. If the killer thought she knew more than me, she could be the next target. I stood on my tip-toes to see over Mary Ann's head. The Thompsons were nowhere in sight.

I fetched Mom and hurried outside. "We need to find Sarah Thompson."

"Why? I need to gather up my dishes before we leave."

"I think she might be the next victim." I strained to see down the street. The sun had not fully set yet, but the couple were nowhere in sight. Instead, the setting sun cast long shadows along the sidewalk and in-between the houses, providing perfect places for someone to hide in wait. "I need to warn her."

"I'll go with you while Ann collects her things," Mary Ann offered.

"No, I need you to tell your brother to check Rusty's apartment for a wall full of photographs."

Her eyebrows rose into her hairline. "Excuse me?"

"He'll see when he goes in there. Come on." I took her hand and set off at a run toward the Thompson house.

A dark van drove past and we dove into the bushes. "Was that Mrs. Henley?"

Mary Ann shrugged. "It could have been the Edgars', I guess. They drive a van. They use it to cart around all the stuff they're clearing out of the house. They said something to Matt about donating most of it to charity. I guess they bought an estate sale, complete with everything in it, including the older model van."

I shook my head and stood. "Come on. We're wasting time."

A scream reverberated from the Thompson's ranch house.

21

Matt dashed past us and banged on the Thompson's front door. Within seconds, it opened and he rushed inside.

Mary Ann and I followed close on his heels, only to be greeted with scowls from both Matt and the Thompsons. "We heard a scream," I said, one hand on my pocket where I kept my Taser.

"Oh, for Pete's sake." Sarah huffed and shook her head. "My imbecile of a husband spilled coffee all over my manuscript. Now, I have to start all over."

Not exactly bad news in my book. "Didn't you save it on your computer?"

"I typed it on a typewriter. After all," She tossed her head, "all the greats were done on a typewriter or by longhand. I want to be like those who have gone before."

Then she needed a different subject matter. "We have reason to believe you may be in danger."

"Stormi," Matt warned. He gave an imperceptible nod of his head, which I chose to ignore. Someone's life might be at stake.

"No, I'm sorry, but I will not be quiet." I

focused a stern look on Sarah. "Regardless of our disagreements, I believe that your talking about research for your novel has put a target on your back. If you know who the killer is, you need to tell Matt. If you don't know, then you need to stop acting as if you do."

"This is the pot calling the kettle black." Sarah crossed her arms. "You're doing the very same thing."

"We're not talking about me."

"Enough." Matt stepped between us. "Both of you need to stop the nonsense and stop messing with a police investigation. Mrs. Thompson, be careful. I'd advise you not to go anywhere alone for a while. Stormi, go home. You, too, Mary Ann."

"Fine." Mary Ann grabbed my arm and dragged me outside. "Let's go to your house."

Once we were inside and helped Mom clean up the pot luck dishes the three of us sat around the table. "Has anyone heard anything from Torie's boyfriend?" Mom asked. "Isn't it suspicious that he's been gone all this time? That the last time he was seen was moments before she was killed? I can't stop thinking about that."

How could I have forgotten about him? Now, not only was Rusty missing in action, but so was the volatile Bob.

A knock on the backdoor sent us all into a screaming fit. Mom and I whipped out our Tasers while Mary Ann hid behind us. Matt walked through the door and shook his head. "Good grief."

"What are you doing here?" Mary Ann resumed her seat.

"Warning the three of you, again, to let me do my job."

"Then you need to take a look at the photos plastered in Rusty's apartment." Since I'd dragged Mary Ann with me to the Thompson house, she hadn't had time to tell her brother of my discovery. "There are tons of them. All of the people in this neighborhood. The victims have been crossed out with a red marker."

His features set into granite. For several seconds, he did nothing but stare stonily at me, most likely piecing together that I was the one who had trespassed in Mrs. Henley's home. I might as well write off any chance of romance with the delectable Matthew Steele. The thought was a knife to the gut.

"Stay here." He whirled and marched out.

"Ooooh, he likes you." Mary Ann wiggles her eyebrows.

"Hardly."

"If he didn't, he would have arrested you just now." She cocked her head. "So, what's our next plan of action? Obviously, we have two, possibly three, main suspects. The Edgars, Mrs. Henley, and Bob. Since Bob is gone, let's focus on the other two and rule them out by process of elimination."

"I can help with that." Angela appeared in the doorway. "The Edgars are here via the Witness Protection Program and will soon be moved because of all the hoopla." She studied her manicure. "My dear little sister disrupts lives wherever she goes."

Not until I'd decided to write a book about the body I stumbled over, but I would let my sister believe what she wanted. It obviously made her feel important. I moved to the front window and peered through a crack in the curtains. "Matt is talking to someone in a dark sedan. That must be the cop he's assigned to watch the house."

"Good deduction, Sherlock." Angela joined me. "That's my boyfriend, Wayne Jones. He volunteered so he could keep me safe."

Good. The man had a vested interest in us, then. Soon after, Matt jogged back to the house and entered through the unlocked front door. Hadn't we learned anything over the last few weeks? I turned and glared at Mom.

She shrugged. "I thought I locked it."

"There are no photos in Rusty's apartment," Matt said.

"Then someone removed them." I sagged onto the sofa. "They were probably gone soon after I found them."

"So, it was you that went into Mrs. Henley's home. Who helped you?"

I clamped my lips shut.

"You are treading on dangerous ground. Who. Helped. You?"

"I did." Dakota stepped into the room. "Aunt Stormi and I make a good team. I'm also the one who found out that old bat served time in jail. Are you going to arrest me?" Despite the belligerent posture in which he stood, shoulders back, arms crossed, I couldn't miss the look of vulnerability in his eyes.

"You dragged my son along with you?" Angela bent over, her face mere inches from mine. "Are you stupid?"

"I made her let me come. If she would have said no, I would have followed her." Dakota plopped down next to me. "There's nothing else to do around here."

She threw her hands up in the air. "This whole family is crazy."

"Who's in the car out front?" Cheyenne sidled through the front door wearing cut off shorts over her bikini. "It's creepy."

"Where have you been?" Angela whirled.

"At the lake." Cheyenne scowled and headed upstairs. "Don't have a conniption fit," she tossed over her shoulder.

"You need to watch your children better." Mom turned and headed for the kitchen.

Matt's mouth opened and closed a few times before he shook his head. "This family is going to kill me." He turned and slammed the front door behind him as he left.

I got off the couch and locked the door. "Now what?"

Mary Ann shrugged. "I'd better go home and prepare myself for a long lecture. I'll call you tomorrow. No more snooping without me, okay? I have a GPS on my phone. That way, if something happens to us, Matt can find us." She flashed a grin, unlocked the door, and followed her brother.

I relocked the door, avoiding my sister's angry looks. "I'm headed to bed. See you tomorrow." With it being Saturday, the entire family would be home. Maybe I'd hole up in my office like a hermit. Oh, how I missed my solitary life.

I headed through my bedroom and into the office to get a clear view of the street. Wouldn't it be more inconspicuous if the detective out front was hidden? Everyone knew every car. Except for the rash of gray vans, that is. Anyone interested would know the police had set Detective Jones up as a lookout.

A light flicked on in Rusty's apartment. The plump figure of Mrs. Henley passed back and forth a couple of times before the light turned off. What could she be looking for? The photos had disappeared, and most likely the notepad. I palmed my forehead. I had completely forgot to tell Matt about the note stating the bad man did it.

Could Rusty be the killer and his guilt-stricken mother covering for him? She'd said many times she would do anything to protect him because of giving him up so many years ago. I turned the blinds to closed.

I was very close to discovering the killer's identity. I knew it in my gut. Ugh. I'd also forgotten to ask Angela why the Edgars' were in protective custody. She wouldn't tell me anything now. Not after dragging her little boy into possible danger.

She was right. I should have locked him in his room rather than let him accompany me. Still, his presence had provided a measure of comfort. I wasn't cut out to be a crime-solver. I was a romance writer! I was in my element writing about hunky heroes and strong women who knew what they wanted out of life.

What did I want? I fell backward across my bed. To be a successful author … check. To own a beautiful home … check. To find a man to grow old with … no check.

Although solving a crime of murder hadn't been on my bucket list, and I'd spent most of the last few weeks scared out of my mind for the safety of my family, I'd gone too far to turn back now. Not to mention the thrill of playing detective. It was like a drug that once taken, stayed in your blood stream. Still, it might be time to take the family on an extended vacation until everything blew over.

I could still finish my book. The crime would be in all the newspapers once it was solved. I could fill in the blanks. I wrote fiction, after all. But the adventure, while dangerous, had brought Mom and I closer than I had ever thought possible. Add in the fact that I didn't want anyone to have to die like my father had, and I thought I had a perfectly good reason for finding the killer.

My whole life had been spent in my older sister's shadow, until I published that first book. Then, everything changed. While Mom still thought Angela needed more attention than I did, I had no longer cared. Which I knew now to be a lie. Mom and I shared a common sense of adventure, and I wasn't ready to let that go.

If only my selfish desire hadn't cost me the possibility of a relationship with Matt. I got up and undressed, then slipped into a short summer nightgown and got under the sheet I covered with in the summer.

Around me, the sounds of the household and neighborhood quieted. Sadie plopped onto her dog bed with a sigh. Ebony and Ivory spread across my feet. No matter what might happen the next day, that night all was right with my world. My family, including the pets, was safe. I'd accomplished, I hoped, what I meant to with the neighborhood meeting. Only time would tell what was to come. I said a prayer for safety and wisdom and closed my eyes.

So much for quiet. Angela shouted some more at Dakota, doors slammed, and footsteps pounded down the hall. Cheyenne added her two cents worth, and Mom said something about waking the neighbors. I shook my head and slapped a pillow over my ears.

Once things seemed to settle down again, I rolled to my back and stared through the dim light at my ceiling. Notes, suspects, and guesses whirled like water down a drain. Certain pieces would slow, then speed back up before I could make sense of them. The killer was right there at the edge of my brain, yet continued to slip out of reach. Wait.

I bolted upright. Had Matt thought to trace the shears that had killed Mrs. Lincoln? Of course, he had. He was a detective. Rusty had once called Bob a bad man. His note stated the bad man did it. Had the police found any evidence of who had ransacked my office shortly after Mom's arrival? Where was Bob?

I searched my memory for anything in Mrs. Lincoln's home or Mrs. Henley's that would fill in a blank. I focused on the women's kitchens and the wood blocks of knives that had set on their counters, a block very similar to the one Mom brought into my house. Mrs. Lincoln's block had been full.

The final piece clicked into place as a gunshot rang out from next door.

22

I met Mom in the hall. "Stay here. Keep Sadie in the house. I'll be right back."

"Take your Taser," she said. "And get that cop out of his car to go with you. I'll call Matt." She grabbed the landline off a hall table. She turned to me, a stricken look on her face. "Phone's dead. I'll try to find a cell phone."

"I think mine is on my bed somewhere." I was pretty sure I fell asleep with it beside me. She would most likely find it tangled in the blanket. "If you can't find it, get yours." I grabbed my Taser, and dashed outside.

Mrs. Henley rushed toward me. "Get in the house," she said. "There's a murderer running loose."

"But the Edgars—"

"They're on their own." She shoved me. "I'm scared out of my mind, Stormi. Get me inside where it's safe."

"Okay, but—" I had distinctly heard a gunshot. "You go on in. I'll be there after I check on them. On second thought, why don't you come with me? There is safety in numbers." No way, did I want her going into my house.

She grabbed my arm and dragged me inside, locking the front door behind us. "Where's the rest of your brood?"

"Upstairs. Why—"

"Stop yapping." She pulled a hand gun from inside her house dress. How could anyone hide a gun in their bra? "Get them all into the kitchen. Now."

"I knew it was you. When I saw the missing knife, well, I didn't realize it then, but I just put the pieces—" She put the gun to my head. I stopped talking and yelled for the others to come downstairs. My heart sank upon hearing their footsteps and complaints at being woken in the middle of the night. Their annoyance was nothing compared to what waited for them in the kitchen.

Tears blurred my vision as one-by-one my family trooped down the stairs and into the kitchen. Mom sniffed and gave Mrs. Henley a look that should have killed her where she stood. "You."

"Well," Mrs. Henley grinned. "Ain't this nice? All together in one place."

"What did you do with the Edgarses?" I stepped in front of Mom.

"They ain't home. Must still be at Bingo."

"But the gunshot."

"I saw my reflection in a mirror and got startled." Her smile didn't fade. "That should show you how unbalanced I am, and how stupid it is for you to keep talking." She motioned for us to take seats at the table.

"My boyfriend," Angela began.

"Is sleeping in his car. Stupid fool. He should know not to take coffee from a killer. Even if that killer is a middle-aged woman." Mrs. Henley laughed. "He'll be out until morning. You," she pointed at Cheyenne, "turn off the lights. We'll sit here by the light of the moon and get to know each other a little better until I take you somewhere far far away. I need to catch my breath. My heart is beating like an Indian drum. How does a permanent vacation to La La Land sound?"

"Where's Bob or Rusty?" I stuffed my Taser between my thighs, pressing them together in the seat to keep it in place, and folded my hands on the table.

"I told you Rusty is at my sister's house. Bob is in jail, the last I heard, for drunken and disorderly conduct. That man does like to party. Oh, cake." She tore off a hunk of carrot cake Mom had baked earlier that day and took a huge bite, raining crumbs down the front of her. "I knew it was just a matter of time before you put the pieces together. Once I found that long hair of yours on my carpet, I knew the gig was up. My dear Rusty was convinced it was a bad person who killed those people. Sad, really, that he saw me, but I was wearing a ski mask and men's clothes. Couldn't hurt him by knowing it was me. I would never hurt that poor boy any more than I already have."

"But, why?" If I kept her distracted enough, could I overpower her and zap her with my Taser? Mom must have been thinking the same thing because she met my gaze and shook her head.

Once Cheyenne turned off the kitchen light,

Angela sat with one arm around each of her children and glared. She showed more fire than I'd ever seen her display. What a sight we must have made, all there in our pajamas and staring down the barrel of a gun.

"Since you're going to kill us anyway," I said, my voice cracking, "may I ask why? Why Mrs. Lincoln? Why Torie?"

"Oh, for crying out loud. You're the nosiest person I've ever met. Can't you just leave it at the fact I had my reasons?" She wiped her free hand on the skirt of her dress. "Marion found out who Rusty's father was. That would have ruined my reputation. All a woman has is her good name, you know. And that slut, Torie, well, she made fun of my boy. Told everyone she knew how he watched her. He couldn't help it!" Spittle flew from her lips. "She taunted him on a daily basis."

"Why do you want to kill Herman and Cecelia?" I shifted my legs to ease the sharp edges of my weapon from digging into my skin.

"They are fugitives, Stormi. Not worth the taxpayer dollars that protect them. Why do you keep squirming?"

"I need to use the restroom."

"Tough. It won't matter soon anyway. Get up. All of you."

"If we leave this house," Mom whispered. "We're dead."

"When I get up, grab my Taser, then shove it into my underpants."

Her eyes widened, but she nodded. "Mine is in my bra."

What was it with fifty-year-old women stuffing weapons into their bras?

"Stop talking." Mrs. Henley rapped me on the shoulder with the butt of the pistol.

My arm went numb, and I cried out. Upstairs, Sadie went crazy barking and clawing at the door. Now, she wanted to be brave, the darling thing. Best she stay where she was. I didn't put it past the crazy woman in front of me to shoot her. Much like she planned for us.

My legs shook as I got to my feet, holding my sore arm close to my side. Before I took a step forward, a cool draft blew up under my nightgown and the cold of the Taser hit my backside. No time for modesty. I'd hike up my skirt and go for the weapon at the first opportunity.

"The van is out front. Move it. Ann, you're driving. One false move and I'll shoot one of your daughters or grandchildren."

"You old witch." Mom shoved past her and outside, leaving the door open and the door banging against the outside wall. "You'll find we won't be as easy to kill as your prior victims. The Nelsons don't go down without a fight."

"We'll see." She held the gun to Dakota's temple. "How's this for incentive?"

Tears welled in his eyes, but to his credit, my nephew didn't make a sound and kept walking. Cheyenne's tears ran down her face, and she huddled close to her mother. I needed to do something before my family was harmed.

I glanced down the street at Matt and Mary Ann's dark house. I wanted to ask Mom if she had ever gotten a call off to Matt, but held my tongue. Either she had or she hadn't. If Matt didn't show up soon, our survival depended on ourselves. Oh, I hoped he showed.

Mrs. Henley ordered Mom to drive, then climbed into the back seat with Dakota, still pointing a gun to his head as incentive for the rest of us to cooperate. Mom reached to grab her seatbelt and laid on the horn. I reached up and turned on the dome light. Lights flickered on up and down the street.

Mrs. Henley whacked me behind my right ear, hard enough to draw blood. I saw stars and clicked off the light. "Stop that horn and drive!"

Mom turned the key and spun tires down the street. "Don't hit my daughter again or I swear I'll drive this van into the nearest light pole and hope you go through the window."

"Tough talk for a dead woman walking." Mrs. Henley leaned over the back of my seat. "Oh, Stormi, you're bleeding. That must hurt like the dickens. Just goes to show what happens when someone messes with me or mine."

I blinked away the colored stars in front of my eyes. For the first time in my life, I strongly desired to hit someone hard enough to knock them out. I squirmed against the hard lump in my underpants. With Mrs. Henley breathing down my neck, there was no way I could retrieve my Taser, not to mention the nausea churning in my stomach from the blow to my head. I didn't know whether to lose consciousness or lose my dinner.

I turned and glanced behind us, hoping, praying,

that my trick with the dome light had alerted one of the neighbors to our predicament. Surely one of them had looked out the window in time to see Mrs. Henley hit me and would contact the police.

Thirty minutes of the longest car ride of my life, Mom turned onto the road that led to the lake. We needed to get away from our abductor. There was only one reason for her to drive us all the way out there in the middle of the night, and it wasn't good.

"Everyone out." Mrs. Henley poked me in the back with her gun. I so wanted to throw the thing out the window.

I scooted across the seat, the Taser scraping my backside, and followed Angela and the kids out the side door. Mom exited and slammed her door, the sound reverberating across the water.

"Keep it up. No one is going to hear you out here. Not at this time of the night. Now start walking."

"Which way? I can't see a thing." Mom turned in a slow circle. "You should have brought a flashlight."

"There's a cave not too far from here, I've heard. Let's go camping. I'm sure one of you brats knows where it is."

"I know," Cheyenne said. "But it will be hard to find in the dark. We'll trip over rocks and roots and stuff."

Mrs. Henley shrugged. "If you fall, I'll shoot you where you lie."

23

"Don't go straight to the cave," I whispered to Cheyenne. "Lead her in a roundabout way." My niece nodded and veered to the right.

"What are you saying up there?" Mrs. Henley huffed her way to my side. "I don't trust you, Stormi. No more talking."

Darn. I'd just been about to reach for my Taser.

I took a step closer to Mom only to have our captor get between us. If I didn't retrieve my Taser soon, I was going to have one heck of a rash, not to mention we were heading deeper into the woods and farther from the van.

I motioned with my head for Mom to hang back as we crested a hill. There was a bit more light, but not much. Heavy clouds skittered across the moon. Add in the fact it was early morning, the darkest hours before dawn, and I could barely see my family beside me. In my white nightgown, I was probably the most visible. Not a good thing when someone wanted to kill you.

I contemplated dashing into the thick trees, yelling run, and hoping my family took the hint and scattered like chickens. The idea might work, having Mrs. Henley focus on me in my stark white rather than the others. I'd rather have her shoot me than any of them. Especially since it was my fault they were all along for the ride. Nosiness really was a new disease for me that I needed to get under control.

What was one more best-seller if it meant my life or the lives of my family? I could just as easily have made up a mystery if that was the route I wanted to take. No one said I needed to experience the plot personally, right? That decision had been mine alone. Mine. Now, my family was at risk. Tears clogged my throat.

The farther we walked, the more I thought skedaddling was the best idea. Why allow ourselves to be led to slaughter like a bunch of old cows? It was better to die fighting, or in this case, running. "Run!"

I dove into the bushes on my left while my sister and her children turned right. I scrambled to my feet and stumbled down what could barely be called a trail. Crashing behind me told me who Mrs. Henley had chosen to pursue me. Good. At least my family was safe.

"Faster, Stormi." Mom panted and gave me a shove from behind. "Here. You dropped this." She shoved my Taser in my hand.

"You weren't supposed to follow me."

"I couldn't let you go alone. Angela has the other two. Move it!" Another shove, then Mom passed me. "Mrs. Henley chose to go after you."

I increased my pace, trying to ignore rocks that cut into my bare feet and branches that tore at my hair. Bruises would heal, bullets were forever. The rest of the family had had time to slide their feet into slippers before coming downstairs. Me? All I'd thought about was getting next door to check on the neighbors. I tripped over an exposed root and wind-milled my arms to keep from falling again and surfed a few feet on slippery, decaying leaves. My dive into the bushes the first time had already taken the skin off my knees, I wasn't in a hurry to add other bruises to my body.

An owl hooted from a tree nearby, sending my heart into my throat. Ahead, I could barely make out the flap of Mom's robe as she passed between the trees.

A shot rang out. Pain ripped through my thigh, sending me to my knees. I screamed and grabbed my leg as I turned to stare into the sweating face of a killer.

Keeping the gun trained on me, Mrs. Henley bent over to catch her breath. "You shouldn't have worn white, you idiot. You stand out like a ghost."

I would have made a smart-mouthed comment about ghosts being invisible if I hadn't been in so much pain. I groaned and flopped to my back. "Just shoot me and get it over with, but leave my family alone." My hand tightened around my Taser. Come closer, come closer.

"I'm sorry, but I can't do that. I'll have to hunt them all down." She leaned against a tree. "I'm not a natural killer, Stormi. You need to believe that."

"Right." Tears streamed down my face. "Killing multiple people comes easy to so many."

She sighed. "You aren't a mother. You don't

understand how a mother feels when someone threatens her child."

"No, but I do." Mom leaped from behind the tree and placed the Taser against Mrs. Henley's neck. The woman let out a sharp shriek and crumbled to the ground. Mom rushed to my side.

"No, not worry about me yet. You only have thirty seconds before she gets up." I pushed to a sitting position. "Use the sash to your robe to tie her up."

"You need it on your leg. You're bleeding pretty bad."

"Mom! Just this once, please listen to me. Hand me her gun and then tie her up." The night seemed to be getting darker. I wasn't sure how much longer I could stay conscious.

Angela and her two, crashed through the brush in time to help Mom drag Mrs. Henley to a tree and tie her arms around the trunk. Dakota pulled off his tee-shirt and tied it around my thigh.

"You've lost a lot of blood, Aunt Stormi." He cinched the tourniquet tight.

I hissed with pain and bit my lip as I flopped onto my back. Matt, where are you? "Someone needs to find their way back to the van and go for help."

"I don't know the way back," Cheyenne admitted. "We took such a long way around, I got us lost."

Wonderful.

"Good. We'll all die out here." Mrs. Henley yanked against her binds. "They'll see me tied to the tree and blame you, Stormi Nelson, writer extraordinaire. The author who will do anything for a story."

"Shut up, you old crow," Mom said, "or I'll zap you again. It will serve you right if a wild animal gets you." She plopped next to me. "We'll wait until daylight and find our way out." She pulled her cell phone from her cleavage.

"What all do you have in there?" I closed my eyes. "It's like a cornucopia."

"This is it. I have one bar on my phone. I'm going to try calling Matt before I lose reception." She punched in a series of numbers. "Hello? Can you hear me? Matthew? We're on the mountain somewhere near the lake... Stormi has been shot ... I don't know where we are, exactly ... We were headed for some cave. My granddaughter managed to get us lost ... Just hurry." She patted my shoulder. "They're going to send a helicopter."

I opened my eyes and stared at the canopy of tree limbs overhead. "Someone needs to find a clearing."

"I'll go." Angela aimed a kick at Mrs. Henley and grabbed Cheyenne's hand. "We'll leave Dakota here to protect you."

"From what?" Mom asked. "The only varmint that wants to kill us is tied up. If she gets undone, I'll zap her again. That felt really good on my end."

I laughed, then groaned. Each movement, no matter how small, sent agony rippling through me. "Wake me when help arrives."

"Oh, no you don't." Mom shook me. "You have to stay awake. If you fall asleep, you'll die. Come on. Scoot up against this log and sit."

Tears streamed down my face as I forced myself into a sitting position. What a baby. Did every person who got shot cry endless tears? I needed something to take my mind off the pain.

"Hey, Mrs. Henley. There are some holes in this mystery that you can fill while we wait. First of all … you used a different weapon each time.

"It's called resourcefulness. A lot of other people could benefit from the same way of thinking."

Mom and I shared a shocked look. "How did you find out the Edgarses were in the Witness Protection?" I asked.

"I didn't. Ethel did. That woman was the biggest snob I'd ever met. Everytime someone new moved into the neighborhood, she Googled them." She tugged against the sash. "I'm not quite sure how she found out Rusty's father was the late, great Harvey Winthrop, but once she confronted me with it, why, I couldn't let her live, now could I?"

Well, yes, she could. "The former mayor Winthrop?"

"I was quite the hottie in my day. My poor husband was infertile, so when I came up pregnant, sparks flew. The poor man had a stroke one day while ranting and raving over my infidelities. I was so distraught that when Rusty was born … special, I put him up for adoption. I never got over that. Untie me this instant!"

With my questions answered, I didn't want to hear her voice for one more second. The woman was pure evil. "Zap her again, Mom. Make her shut up."

"Gladly." Mom zapped her and tightened the sash while Mrs. Henley sat slumped over. "A few more minutes and she would have been free. I'm not that good at tying knots after all."

"Here." Dakota whipped the drawstring from his shorts. "We can tie her feet with this."

Without the string, his shorts hung dangerously low. Good thing we wouldn't need to run anymore or my nephew would be sporting nothing but a pair of boxers. "I love you, Dakota," I said, "you're a great kid to go sleuthing with."

He cast a worried glance at Mom. "Uh, I love you, too. Is she dying?"

Mom shook her head. "Just delirious from blood loss."

Despite the bravery in Mom's words, I could tell she was worried. If Matt didn't arrive soon, I might not get to write the ending to my story. The world faded, and my eyes closed.

*

I woke to movement that sent shards of glass through me. I opened my eyes and stared at the firm jawline of the hunky Matthew Steele. "You came."

He glanced down. "Nothing could have kept me away."

"I thought you were mad at me."

"No, I only wanted you to be safe, you silly, foolish woman." He shifted my weight, cradling me closer to his chest. "We'll be at the copter soon. You're going to be fine."

"I'm feeling a bit weak." If God was going to call me home, there was nowhere I'd rather spend my last moments than in Matt's arms. "I see a light." This was it. This was the end.

"That's the light on the copter."

"Oh." I buried my face in his neck and closed my mouth before I said something embarrassing.

Soon, we were airborne, me strapped to a gurney and Matt sitting beside me. "Your family will meet us at the hospital," he said. "Mrs. Henley is on her way to jail. I have your Taser."

"It was down my underpants, but it fell out."

His eyes widened, but he wisely chose not to ask any questions about why I had carried it there. I suppose it might have been mortifying had I managed to zap myself. I was delirious. No doubt about it. Matt had saved my life, chose to ride in the copter with me despite his earlier threat to spend no more time in my company, and I talked about stupid things. Instead, I should be telling him my feelings, and making promises to never go against his advice again.

I'd just made up my mind to say so, when the paramedic put an oxygen mask on my face. My leg throbbed, I was freezing, and my brain refused to focus. Maybe I really was dying, and Mrs. Henley could add another murder to her belt.

I lost consciousness again, not opening my eyes until I was in the hospital. Mom slept in a chair on one side of my bed, and Matt slumped in the other. I wanted a drink of water more than almost anything in the world. I groaned and reached for the nurse's button.

"Hey." Matt stood and grabbed the water pitcher beside the bed. He poured water into a plastic cup and inserted one of those bendable straws before lifting it to my mouth. "How are you feeling?"

"Like I was shot." I pursed my lips around the straw. The water was pure nectar from heaven.

"You've slept for three days. The doctors had to give you a blood transfusion, which your sister gladly offered to donate."

Great. She would never let me live down the fact that she saved my life. "How long has Mom been here?"

"Off and on the entire time."

Mom stirred and opened her eyes. "No more than he has. I sure am glad to see you awake, daughter. I thought for a while there we might lose you."

"I thought the same. God must have had other plans." I held out my hands, taking theirs in mine. "Thank you. But, I'm going to be okay. You should go home now and get some proper rest."

They shook their heads like moving bookends. "Now that you're awake," Mom said, "you'll most likely be released tomorrow. I'm sure we can hold it together that long." She released my hand and sat back in her seat.

Matt kept his grasp on mine and pulled his chair closer to the bed. "Mrs. Henley confessed to the murders. Rusty will stay with her sister indefinitely. She also confessed to having a history of mental illness and not taking her meds because they upset her stomach."

Mental illness wasn't a surprise. "I guess I've lost my gardener." I'd miss the neighborhood Peeping Tom. "Does he understand what has happened?"

"Nothing more than that Mrs. Henley died." Matt sighed and rubbed his chin. "Ann, may I have a moment alone with Stormi?"

"Oh, sure." Mom jumped to her feet. "I could use some coffee." She winked and left.

Matt glued his gaze to mine, the pain and anguish flittering across his eyes brought tears to mine. What had happened? Maybe my family didn't all make it home. "What? Did someone die?"

"No, everyone is fine. I'm so sorry I wasn't there to save you."

"But you did save me. You found us." I put my other hand over the one he held, the one with the IV needle creating its own brand of torture for my body. "If you hadn't gotten there when you did, I would have bled to death. Thank God, Mom called you."

"I was already on my way. The Edgarses were returning home and saw Mrs. Henley in the van with you and their foyer mirror shattered. They came looking for me the same time as Mr. Olson who looked out his window when he heard a horn honking. We put the pieces together, what with the bullet hole in the Edgars' wall and your house dark with the doors wide open and Sadie barking loud enough to raise the dead." His eyes misted over. "It wasn't until your Mom called though, that we had a better idea of where to look.

"Your sister flagged down the copter and we were able to trace her steps back to you. When I saw you lying on the ground, your gown soaked with blood and your Mom crying …" His shoulders shook. "I thought I was too late." He laid his cheek against the hand with the IV, taking care not to knock the needle.

"I was feeling a little woozy." I smiled and placed a hand on his head. The wheat-colored strands were soft and thick to my touch. I ran my fingers through his hair. "You're going to love how I portray you in my book."

"Oh, no." He groaned and lifted his head. "Seriously?"

I nodded. "If you aren't still mad at me, do you think you would mind very much volunteering to help me research the love scenes?"

He grinned, a dimple winking in his right cheek. "Now, that, I'm looking forward to."

24

Two weeks after returning home, the constant company of my family hovering over me cast a pall of suffocation. I stared at the crutches in the corner, close enough at hand, I could leave if I wanted to, but Matt had just arrived. Very few things could make me flee *his* company.

He planted a tender kiss on my forehead, then a more intimate one on my lips that made me forget about the healing throb in my thigh. "Hey." His husky greeting washed over me like a gentle rain.

"Hey." I puckered for another kiss, which he gave before sitting next to me on the loveseat and pulling me under his arm. I snuggled in and breathed deep of Matt.

"Mrs. Henley's hearing is next week. I think it's a good idea for all of you to go. The evidence against her is overwhelming, but it never hurts the judge to see the living victims, especially young people."

I nodded. "We'll be there. I'm hoping they'll put her away for a long time."

"For life, most likely." He rubbed my bare arm, his touch as soothing as a favorite silk blouse. "Are you going stir-crazy yet?"

"No, I've spent most of my time writing. My agent, while relieved my research didn't result in my death, is ecstatic at my progress. The book should be done by the end of summer." I couldn't wait. The title, *Anything for a Story*, couldn't be more perfect.

"Have you had your fill of solving murders?" He gave me a gentle squeeze.

"I think so." I chuckled. "After all, how many times can there be a murder in a peaceful subdivision like Oak Meadows?"

Mom laughed as she entered the room. She set a tray of tea and cookies on the coffee table. "If there is one, you'll stumble over it. I have to admit, I'll miss the excitement."

"Maybe you can join the Edgarses for Bingo on Friday nights," I suggested with a grin.

"Heaven forbid. I'm not that old."

"Mom needs a man," Angela said, studying her nails. "Dating Wayne has really brightened up my life."

Cheyenne rolled her eyes and continued texting away on her phone. "No mushy stuff or I'm out of here."

I glanced around at the faces of everyone I loved. Even Cheyenne's pretty but surly teenage face couldn't dispel my mood. If only they didn't feel the need to be around me every waking moment. Finding solitude to write had become more than enough of a challenge for me. But, I was grateful for my family. Having had to go through what I did alone would have been ten times more horrifying, yet I still wished they hadn't had to experience the adventure.

Matt put his ears close to mine, his breath tickling my neck. "Want to research a kissing scene?"

"Oh, gross." Cheyenne pushed to her feet and stomped from the room. Dakota grinned and followed his sister, Mom and Angela also taking the hint.

I tilted my face to his. "I'm hoping to research a lot with you. You're the perfect novel hero."

His mouth quirked at one corner. "I'm not sure about the hero part, but I think more research can be arranged." He lowered his head and claimed my lips.

Yep, the danger was all worth it if it meant I had this handsome man at my side. I couldn't help but wonder, and look forward to, whatever came next.

The End

Dear Reader:

Thank you so much for reading Anything for a Mystery. I hope you fell in love with these characters as much as I did. There are six more books to enjoy. Below is the first chapter of book two, A Killer Plot.

Reviews are extremely important to an author. If you enjoyed Anything for a Mystery, please leave a review here, it's super easy.

If you want to keep up with my new releases, please sign up for my newsletter here and receive a free story.

I've also got some other fun and quirky mysteries. Fudge-Laced Felonies is book one in the Summer Meadows Mysteries and features Summer Meadows, a fun-loving candy store owner on a mission to find a killer.

In Deadly Neighbors, book one in the River Valley Mysteries, Marsha Steele is out to find the person poisoning and robbing the town's residents before she becomes a victim herself.

In the Shady Acres series, book one, Beware the Orchids, Shelby Jenkins starts her new job as gardener in an upscale retirement community and stumbles across a dead body. Full of quirky characters it is sure to please cozy mystery fans.

In the Hollywood Murder Mysteries, Kelly Canyon, Paparazzi extraordinaire, gets roped into an acting gig and straight into murder.

Enjoy the first chapter of A Killer Plot.

1

"How does it feel to be on the NYT Best Seller's list again?" My agent, Elizabeth Swanson, asked.

"Just as wonderful as the first time." Few things were better than seeing my name, Stormi Nelson, on the cover of a book. I sipped my coffee and watched my Irish Wolf Hound, Sadie, chase a squirrel across the yard. After the murders six months ago, and the publication of my first mystery novel, I relished the peace.

"How is your hunky hero?"

"He's been on an undercover assignment for a few months. I'm lucky if I get a phone call from him." Not to mention how much I missed his kisses. After all, I'd designed the hero in my book after him.

"Have you started the next book in the series?"

"I'm waiting for inspiration." Which arrived daily in the form of ever-increasingly disturbing emails. Something I chose to keep to myself at the moment. "I'll keep you updated. Bye."

I hung up, dropped the phone on the table next to me and studied the email I had received that morning from "Your biggest fan".

"Miss Nelson, I continue to anxiously await your next novel and book signing. Maybe I should help move things along for you? I have certain talents that will help take your mystery writing to the next level. If I don't see a second book soon, I'm afraid I'll have to implement some serious action."

I shuddered. The latest email might not be cause for alarm, if not for all the ones prior. I received one a day from this person, and after answering the first one and letting the sender know it would be well into the next year before a new manuscript would be finished, I'd stopped answering.

"Come on, Sadie." I stood and held the kitchen door open. Sadie bounded inside, almost knocking Mom over in her haste.

"Gracious, that dog is like a bull dozer." Mom set a plate of pancakes on the table. "I wish I had her energy."

"Me, too." I grabbed a pancake, and carrying the disc of fluffy fried batter, headed to my office to start the writing day.

While I ate, I booted up my laptop. Feet pounded down the stairs outside my office. My nephew, Dakota, and niece, Cherokee, were running late for school, as usual. They spent more time in sweep at the high school than they did in class, it seemed. Their mother, Angela, should make sure they're up before she headed to her job as receptionist at the local police station. Still, it wasn't my place to judge.

My laptop came to life and alerted me to another email. The blood drained from my head to my feet as I discovered it was from my biggest fan. Was the person going to email me every hour from now on? I really needed to let Matt know the next time he called. Maybe he could trace the emails somehow and tell the person to layoff.

Speaking of phone calls, I'd left my cell phone outside. Getting out of my chair, I yelled for Mom to bring me the phone when she had a minute. Distractions of one sort or another kept me from actually starting my writing until eight a.m. each morning. That gave me ten more minutes to piddle around until the house quieted down.

"Here you go." Mom pushed open the door and tossed me the phone. "I'm headed out for supplies. A lot of orders to fill."

Mom had started an in-home bakery three months ago and, to my surprise, worked very diligently filling orders. Someday, maybe she could actually have her own bakery and I could have my kitchen back. I felt as if I rarely got to relax by cooking anymore.

"Thank you." I checked for messages from Matt. Nothing. I sighed and settled back into my chair, fingers poised over the keyboard. I needed to write a minimum of three thousand words to stay on track of finishing a rough draft in less than two months.

Two hours and the first chapter done, I was well on my way to a juicy little murder. I'd chosen the crime of, A Killer Plot, to be about an author cyber-stalked by a fanatic fan. A bit close for comfort, considering I'd received two more emails, one an hour, from my very own stalker, but the annoying emails needed to be good for something, right? Why not fodder for a new book? It might be just the thing I needed to avoid an all-out fear fest.

I saved the manuscript and headed to the kitchen

for lunch, sticking my phone in the pocket of my new skinny jeans. Matt hadn't called in over a week. Today might be the day he called and erased my worry about him.

Mom had a rack of cupcakes cooling on the table and filled another pan with batter. "I haven't fixed lunch, yet. Sorry."

"I can fix myself a sandwich. I know you're busy."

"Haven't bought groceries, either."

I sighed. Hadn't she said earlier that she was headed to the store? "No problem. I'll go." I grabbed my purse from next to the refrigerator and grabbed the never-ending list of groceries my family couldn't, or wouldn't, live without. I really needed to start charging people rent.

Once behind the wheel of my Mercedes, I backed out of the driveway and headed to the grocery store. I filled my shopping cart with almost everything on the list, how many candy bars did a teenager need anyway? And got in the long line by the cashier.

"Stormi, it's good to see you." Sarah Thompson, local erotic and horror novel writer, tapped me on the shoulder. "It's been so long, you haven't seen my newest work."

I didn't want to either. The last I'd read had given me nightmares for a week. My neighbor definitely had a twisted mind, and the writing wasn't very good either. "How's the self-publishing business?"

"Booming. There's a real market for steamy stuff. You really should change genres."

I fought back a shudder. "I'm having too much fun to change." My bank account wasn't suffering much either.

"It's a lot more fun to research murder, mayhem, and deviant acts." Sarah wiggled her eyebrows. "Oh, but you're man has been away for a while, hasn't he? You poor thing."

Thankfully, the cashier motioned me forward, saving me from having to answer. At one time, I'd suspected Sarah of being a murderer. After all, she'd said she'd do anything for a story, and her last book had followed the crimes happening in Oak Meadow Estates to a Tee. Still, it had also given me plenty to write about and landed me at number five on the NYT Best Selling list. Write about what you know, right? Since I had been the one to stumble across the first dead body, I'd had plenty of words to put to paper.

"That will be two hundred dollars and thirty-six cents," the cashier said.

I definitely needed to charge my family rent. I pushed my heavy cart back out to the car.

Bill Olsen waved a hand in greeting. His wife, Norma, promptly shoved him away from me and toward the store. The woman's jealousy hadn't dissipated one iota. I grinned. Maybe some women found older, balding, paunchy men attractive, but I was happy with my hunky detective. Now, if he would only call. Matt, not Bill.

Trunk full of food I wouldn't have to buy if I still lived alone, I drove home, unloaded and put away the groceries, and let Sadie into the yard to run. I watched for a few minutes, then filched one of Mom's cupcakes. "Oh, filling!"

Mom glared. "I only made enough extras for each of the family to have one. Don't think you'll get another one tonight when everyone else is enjoying theirs."

"As if Angela would risk the extra calories." I would get my sister's for sure. "Who are these for?"

"The Women's Auxiliary at the church is having a bake sale. They paid me fifty dollars to make two hundred of these to sell." Mom chuckled. "I would have made them for free."

"No sense if they're willing to pay." I took another bite and bit back a moan. "You are a baking genius." Maybe I could help set my mother up in her own shop. I had the money. They could be partners, with me handling the financial aspect.

My pocket vibrated, alerting me to a call. I dug the cell phone out and dashed to the back porch and privacy. "Matt."

"Hey, sweetheart."

"I've missed you." I plopped onto a lawn chair. "When are you coming home?"

"A few more days, I promise. How are things over there?"

I almost told him about my cyber-stalker, but hesitated. He had enough to worry about. "I've started my next book, which will make my agent happy. I could use some research help for the love scenes."

"I'm looking forward to it."

His husky voice sent my pulse racing. "I'm thinking about funding Mom's bakery."

"That's sweet of you."

I grinned. "Her birthday is tomorrow. I'll tell her then. She's amazing, Matt. I've gained five pounds since she started this venture."

"In all the right places, I bet."

"Maybe." And maybe not. My pants had grown a bit snug. I closed my eyes and leaned against the chair back. "Are you staying safe?"

"As much as I'm able. Look, baby, I've got to go. Take care of yourself, okay?"

"You, too." Tears pricked my eyes as I said goodbye and sent up a prayer for his safety. Less than a year ago, I hadn't known he existed, now he filled my heart. Six months was a long time for him to be undercover. Each day, each week, that passed filled me with dread. Each sight of a squad car driving down the street left me cold.

"Hey, Aunt Stormi." Dakota joined me on the porch, handing me a cold diet soda. "Things aren't the same out here without a murder, are they?"

"Don't tell me you're missing a nighttime hike at gunpoint." I popped the soda tab.

"Maybe a little." He grinned and guzzled his soda. "The good thing is it brought us all closer together, don't you think."

I clapped a hand on his knee. "I know it did. I might have grumbled at first when y'all moved in, disrupting my quiet life, but I prefer the occasional bouts of noise." To my surprise, I truly did. Living alone had been a miserable existence. Now, instead of living between the pages of my novels, I actually lived. "Now, to get your sister and you to stop fighting and get to school on time."

"Doubt that will happen." He finished his drink

and crushed the can in his hand. "I've got football practice. See you at supper." He bounded away with all the energy of a sixteen-year-old.

I sighed and transferred my attention to Sadie digging under a hydrangea bush. "Sadie, stop that." When the dog ignored me, I pushed off the chair and went to investigate. "I've spent a lot of money on this landscaping, you scoundrel. No digging." I grabbed the dog's collar.

Sadie pulled against my grasp. In the dirt, lay a new rawhide bone, still clean and pristine against the mulch. "Where did that come from?" I picked it up.

"Flowers." Mom called from the house. "Just arrived for you."

Matt! I dashed toward the house, dropping the bone in the garbage on the way.

On the kitchen table sat a bouquet of spring flowers. I grabbed the note and tore open the envelope.

"Does your dog like my gift? Careful. You shouldn't take treats from a stranger."

Connect with me on FaceBook
Twitter
Bookbub
Sign up for my newsletter and receive a free short story
www.cynthiahickey.com

Follow me on Amazon

Enjoy other books by Cynthia Hickey

Time Travel
The Portal

A Hollywood Murder
Killer Pose, book 1
Killer Snapshot, book 2

Shady Acres Mysteries
Beware the Orchids, book 1
Path to Nowhere
Poison Foliage
Poinsettia Madness
Deadly Greenhouse Gases
Vine Entrapment

CLEAN BUT GRITTY

Highland Springs

Murder Live
Say Bye to Mommy
To Breathe Again

Colors of Evil Series

Shades of Crimson
Coral Shadows

The Pretty Must Die Series

Ripped in Red, book 1

Pierced in Pink, book 2
Wounded in White, book 3
Worthy, The Complete Story

Lisa Paxton Mystery Series

Eenie Meenie Miny Mo
Jack Be Nimble
Hickory Dickory Dock

One Hour (A short story thriller)

INSPIRATIONAL
(scroll down to see clean books without inspirational message)

Whisper Sweet Nothings (a short romance)

Nosy Neighbor Series
Anything For A Mystery, Book 1
A Killer Plot, Book 2
Skin Care Can Be Murder, Book 3
Death By Baking, Book 4
Jogging Is Bad For Your Health, Book 5
Poison Bubbles, Book 6
A Good Party Can Kill You, Book 7 (Final)
Nosy Neighbor collection

Christmas with Stormi Nelson

The Summer Meadows Series
Fudge-Laced Felonies, Book 1

Candy-Coated Secrets, Book 2
Chocolate-Covered Crime, Book 3
Maui Macadamia Madness, Book 4
All four novels in one collection

The River Valley Mystery Series
Deadly Neighbors, Book 1
Advance Notice, Book 2
The Librarian's Last Chapter, Book 3
All three novels in one collection

Historical cozy
Hazel's Quest

Historical Romances
Runaway Sue
Taming the Sheriff
Sweet Apple Blossom

Finding Love the Harvey Girl Way
Cooking With Love
Guiding With Love
Serving With Love
Warring With Love
All 4 in 1

A Wild Horse Pass Novel
They Call Her Mrs. Sheriff, book 1 (A Western Romance)

Finding Love in Disaster

The Rancher's Dilemma
The Teacher's Rescue
The Soldier's Redemption

Woman of courage Series

A Love For Delicious
Ruth's Redemption
Charity's Gold Rush
Mountain Redemption
Woman of Courage series (all four books)

Short Story Westerns
Desert Rose
Desert Lilly
Desert Belle
Desert Daisy
Flowers of the Desert 4 in 1

Romantic Suspense

Overcoming Evil series
Mistaken Assassin
Captured Innocence
Mountain of Fear
Exposure at Sea
A Secret to Die for
Collision Course
Romantic Suspense of 5 books in 1

The Game
Suspicious Minds

Contemporary

Romance in Paradise
Maui Magic
Sunset Kisses
Deep Sea Love
3 in 1

Finding a Way Home

Service of Love

Christmas

Handcarved Christmas
The Payback Bride
Curtain Calls and Christmas Wishes
Christmas Gold
A Christmas Stamp
Snowflake Kisses

The Red Hat's Club (Contemporary novellas)

Finally
Suddenly
Surprisingly
The Red Hat's Club 3 – in 1

Short Story

One Hour (A short story thriller)
Whisper Sweet Nothings (a Valentine short

romance)

Made in United States
Orlando, FL
14 March 2022